And then just like that, Katie was in his arms again.

He held her, resting his head lightly atop hers. He could feel her heartbeat. He could smell her shampoo. And it was all back, those unexpected feelings he'd had yesterday in the attic.

Wanting her.

She was so close. She looked up at him, her pink-red plush lips so inviting and he leaned down slightly and kissed her, which sent blood coursing through every part of his body. She deepened the kiss to the point that there was no stepping back.

His hands were in her hair, on her sweater, moving under her sweater. He felt her hands snake around his neck, her lips on his neck. They tumbled onto the bed and he shoved off the empty suitcase.

It was only when the suitcase hit the floor with a thud that Asher froze, his hands slowly untwining from Katie's silky hair, his lips gone from hers. One minute he'd been lying on top of her, and now he was standing up, the air out of his lungs.

"I got caught in the moment," he whispered. "I'm sorry."

"We got caught up in the moment. And maybe the moment is a natural progression, Asher. It clearly is or we wouldn't be here...again, right?"

Dear Reader,

Last Christmas, rookie police officer Katie Crosby was forced to fake her own death to save the lives of those she loved, including rancher Asher Dawson, her best friend since childhood and the man she's secretly loved forever. She had to "disappear" knowing that she was pregnant with Asher's twins from an unexpected night of passion.

This Christmas, however, Katie can finally come home to Bear Ridge, Wyoming, with her baby boys— and reunite with Asher. A lot has changed but Asher's heart is as off-limits to her as ever, even as they marry for the sake of the twins...

I hope you enjoy Asher and Katie's love story. I love to hear from readers, so feel free to email me with your thoughts about *Santa's Twin Surprise*. You can find more information about all my books at my website: MelissaSenate.com.

Happy holidays!

Melissa Senate

Santa's Twin Surprise

MELISSA SENATE

HARLEQUIN
SPECIAL
EDITION

HARLEQUIN®
SPECIAL EDITION™

Recycling programs
for this product may
not exist in your area.

ISBN-13: 978-1-335-72427-4

Santa's Twin Surprise

Copyright © 2022 by Melissa Senate

For questions and comments about the quality of this book,
please contact us at CustomerService@Harlequin.com.

Harlequin Enterprises ULC
22 Adelaide St. West, 41st Floor
Toronto, Ontario M5H 4E3, Canada
www.Harlequin.com

Printed in U.S.A.

Melissa Senate has written many novels for Harlequin and other publishers, including her debut, *See Jane Date*, which was made into a TV movie. She also wrote seven books for Harlequin Special Edition under the pen name Meg Maxwell. Her novels have been published in over twenty-five countries. Melissa lives on the coast of Maine with her teenage son; their rescue shepherd mix, Flash; and a lap cat named Cleo. For more information, please visit her website, melissasenate.com.

Books by Melissa Senate

Harlequin Special Edition

Dawson Family Ranch

For the Twins' Sake
Wyoming Special Delivery
A Family for a Week
The Long-Awaited Christmas Wish
Wyoming Cinderella
Wyoming Matchmaker
His Baby No Matter What
Heir to the Ranch

The Wyoming Multiples

The Baby Switch!
Detective Barelli's Legendary Triplets
Wyoming Christmas Surprise
To Keep Her Baby
A Promise for the Twins
A Wyoming Christmas to Remember

Furever Yours

A New Leash on Love
Home is Where the Hound Is

Visit the Author Profile page
at Harlequin.com for more titles.

In memory of my dear grandmother.

Chapter One

Christmas used to be Asher Dawson's favorite time of year. *This* Christmas he could barely look at a lit-up shop window without wanting to get back into bed, pull the blanket over his head and not emerge till January.

Everything about the season reminded him of Katie. The best friend he'd ever had.

Right now, as he stood in front of the decorated tree on the town green, he thought about the time he and Katie played trees in the kindergarten holiday play, both of them wrapped in red tinsel with silver stars they'd made out of construction paper on their heads. This morning, when he'd gone into town for breakfast, the multicolored lights on the windows had reminded him of when Katie, just eighteen and aged out of her group foster home, had moved into her first apartment, a studio above the laundromat, and he'd surprised her by stringing lights around her door. Even the music in the diner while he'd had his pancakes and coffee had his chest aching at the memory of Katie singing along to "Santa Claus Is Coming to Town" on the radio in his red pickup—just days before he'd lost her.

And because it was unseasonably warm today for Wyoming in December, a beautiful fifty-two degrees, many of those who'd come out for the holiday event in the park were wearing only Christmas sweaters, flashing him back to his and Katie's long-standing competition of finding the goofiest possible one to wear on Christmas Day. Last December, he'd found a bright red-and-green fuzzy one with a cartoon moose made up of working tiny lights, the small switch at the neck really uncomfortable but worth it. And he'd won, of course.

Then lost everything.

Katie Crosby was gone the day after Christmas.

As people milled around, trying to get closer to the tree, taking photos, singing along to the group of carolers by the Santa hut, he wondered why he thought he could do this. Be here. Be part of this.

"You all right, Ash?" his cousin Ford asked from beside him.

Nope, Asher thought. Not all right. But he was here, trying.

"Gotta be hard," his other cousin Rex said, slinging an arm around his shoulder.

Hard didn't begin to cover what this was.

"I'm okay," he told them. He glanced around. "Good crowd today," he added to get the subject off him. There must have been three hundred people gathered around the tree. Bear Ridge was sponsoring a Secret Santa Wish Request. Anyone could write down an anonymous Christmas wish and drop it in a box in the town hall, and the holiday committee had created little plastic pouches to hang on the tree containing those wishes. Today, residents would take a request and fulfill it, then bring the gift to the town hall where it would be matched with the recipient via a corresponding number. The Secret Santa event was hosted by the Bear Ridge Police Department, where Ford and Rex were both officers.

Where Katie had been a rookie. Ford had been her training partner, and Asher knew his cousin had taken the loss particularly hard.

The accident, on a snowy, curvy mountain road the day after Christmas last year, felt like yesterday and forever ago. Yesterday for how raw the grief felt. Forever for how much Asher missed the woman he'd known since he was five. The best friend who'd do anything for him—even agree to marry him, platonically, for a year so he could inherit his grandmother's ranch.

In his grief and desperation over the loss of his beloved gram a year ago last November, he'd proposed the deal to Katie. She'd said she'd have to think about it, then five seconds later said yes, of course she'd help him out. His grandmother's funeral, the reading of the will, asking Katie to give up a year of her life for him, the idea of getting married, even platonically, had all done a number on him. His family, friends, people he barely knew in town had been congratulating him on his engagement, no idea about the terms of the will, and suddenly the enormity of what he'd proposed—the idea of actually getting married and to Katie in some crazy arrangement—had sunk in. He'd had a few drinks at the bar where he and Katie liked to play darts, then texted her. He'd figured they'd talk it over a little more. Instead, they'd both had too much to drink.

And had ended up in bed.

Maybe after this the marriage will be real, Katie had whispered naked beside him before she'd fallen asleep. And he'd lain there, eyes wide-open, staring at the ceiling in a panic. She'd been very tipsy, of course, so maybe she hadn't meant it.

But he couldn't stop thinking about what she'd said. Twenty minutes of ruminating and staring out the window at the inky night, and he'd been stone-cold sober. He'd quickly gotten dressed in a kind of panic, Katie suddenly sitting up and catching him trying to quietly slip out the door. It had been so awkward. The terrible conversation about how they were drunk, that it was a mistake, Katie nodding and turning away, pulling the blanket up to her chin. They'd avoided each other for a month until she'd come to the ranch on Christmas Eve, found him in the barn milking Minnie and told him they'd been friends for twenty-five years and could get through anything, even a drunken night of wild sex that *he'd* clearly regretted.

That part had stuck with him for the next couple of days. So she hadn't regretted it? She'd meant what she'd said about the marriage being real? He hadn't wanted to think about that, or what she'd said before she'd fallen asleep.

Instead, he'd hugged her hard and then they were back, best friends. There'd been a lot going on then, in both their lives, and they'd needed each other, as they'd always had. Wearing their ugly sweaters, they'd spent Christmas Eve together like always and Christmas Day with his Dawson cousins at their dude ranch since both his parents, long divorced and on their third and fourth marriages, had other plans, and his grandmother was gone. Neither mentioned the night they'd shared. Or the marriage proposal. But his cousins and their spouses kept asking about the marriage plans, and Asher had gone quieter and quieter as the evening wore on.

By the next morning, he'd known he couldn't marry Katie, couldn't ask her to give up her life for a year, couldn't risk their friendship again. What had been clear to *him* was that she could see them truly together. Marriage—even on a platonic deal for a year—would get complicated. *They* were both complicated. So he'd taken back the proposal.

That conversation had been even worse than the awkward middle-of-the-night escape from her bedroom. But he'd never had a chance to explain better. That he loved her too much, cared about her too much to put her in such a position for an entire year of her life. She'd run out, driving off in the snow that had started coming down hard. It was the last time he'd seen her.

And now here he was a year later, the deadline looming to marry by this December 25 or lose the ranch and Asher having no intention of doing anything about it, as he hadn't for the past year.

He had to sell his grandmother's small ranch and dairy business whether he liked it or not, and he didn't like it. Not one bit. There was already a for-sale sign at the front gate and on the road where the turnoff was to the property. The sight of those signs always made his chest constrict. But he had no choice. He wasn't going to marry anyone else. He'd messed up—bad—and that was that.

"I feel like someone is kicking me hard in the chest," Asher found himself saying, shoving his hands in the pockets of his down jacket. "But maybe that's a good thing. At least I'm feeling something." No one, not even his cousins, had known about the stipulation in his grandmother's will. That he'd proposed because of it. That'd he ended the engagement. He'd wanted to shout from the barn roof that he was a fraud.

This time Ford slung an arm around his shoulder. "We all miss her so much," he said. "The town wish request was her idea. She'd be touched to know we were doing it. And that you're a part of it even though it's rough on you."

That made him feel better. Asher had helped Ford and Rex hang the little wish holders around the tree like ornaments, and he'd actually agreed to take on a few shifts as the town Santa in the Christmas hut a few feet away because he and Katie had done it every year and he had to do it for her. She'd loved sitting on the big red velvet chair in her Santa costume with the line of children outside, listening to their wishes, telling them she knew they'd tried to be good and that counted.

Her face flashed into his mind. The pale brown

eyes, brown chin-length hair, the freckles across her cheeks that she'd always complained about. God, he missed her. His grandmother had always asked when he and Katie were going to realize they were meant to be. He'd tried to explain that they were meant to be best friends but his gram would scowl and wave her arm around. More than once his grandmother had said he should look beyond the "plain-Jane tomboy," as Katie had always referred to herself, to see what was really important. His grandmother had never warmed to any of his girlfriends, who maybe had been on the flashy side in heels and makeup. He'd always thought Katie was the loveliest person he'd ever known, inside and out, but he'd only ever seen her as his best friend. Which he'd always thought was a good thing, since no matter who'd flitted in and out of his life over the decades in long and short romances, she was the one constant in his life. With parents who'd had multiple marriages, stepparents in and out of his life, constancy meant something to Asher.

He'd almost messed up after they'd slept together. Then he had messed it up for good the night he'd told her the proposal was off the table.

"Asher, you should know something," Ford said, his blue eyes intense. "The Bear Ridge PD got word this morning that the ex-con who'd threatened Katie, and who might have had something to do with her accident, was killed yesterday in an armed robbery two hours north of here."

Asher dropped his head back. He didn't want to think of that ex-con at all. Last Christmas Eve, Katie had been threatened by a thief she'd arrested and testified against; the woman had gotten off on a technicality and vowed to kill everyone Katie loved. Katie, still a rookie, had been terrified, but her colleagues had rallied and worked around the clock to find the woman who'd hid out too well, and Asher hadn't left her side, the worry giving them something to focus on besides the strain between them. When Christmas had come and gone without incident, everyone had breathed a sigh of relief.

But that next night, faint tire marks on the snowy road had indicated the possibility that a second car had been the reason Katie's car had struck the guardrail on a curve in the road and gone over the cliff. The ex-con? No one had known for sure and she'd seemed to disappear. Katie's car had been found in the Bear Ridge River, her body never recovered.

And Asher had blamed himself. She shouldn't have been alone until that woman was caught, but because of him, she'd driven off in the falling snow before he could stop her. He'd gone after her, to make sure she'd gotten home okay. But when he'd arrived at her apartment in town, her car hadn't been there. It hadn't been at the bar they liked. Or at any of her girlfriends' places. So he'd called Ford and asked him to keep an eye out. It was Ford who'd noticed the smashed guardrail, shattered glass from a car windshield at the cliff below and Katie's shoulder bag and red mittens found hours later half in the river, half tangled on a rock at the shoreline. However the accident had happened, because of the weather or because of the ex-con, Katie Crosby was lost to him.

Asher closed his eyes for a moment, trying to shake himself of the memories that had haunted him for nearly a year. He forced himself to watch a happy family—a set of parents and a little boy around six or seven years old—taking photos in front of the tree. The kid wore a Santa hat just like Asher, Ford and Rex with Bear Ridge, WY, embroidered on it. The hats were free at the town hall. It had taken a lot to shove the thing on his head before getting out of his SUV. The dad asked Asher if he'd take a family photo, and Asher said sure and took two just in case his focus was off, which of course it was these days.

As he handed back the phone, the little boy sidled next to him and raised his hand.

Asher smiled. "You have a question for me?"

The boy nodded. "Should I tell Santa what I want for Christmas if I already have a wish on the tree?"

"Sure," Asher said. "This way you have double the chance of getting your Christmas wish."

The smile that broke out on the boy's face almost had Asher remembering how sweet and innocent Christmas had once seemed. The huge turkey dinner, basically a repeat of Thanksgiving, and cups of spiked egg nog and way too many gifts under the tree at his grandmother's ranch, Katie coming every year since she didn't have family of her own. Even when he was a kid his parents would go out of town with a new significant other or spouse for major holidays. His grandmother and Katie had been the only constants. Now they were both gone.

As Asher watched the boy race back to his parents, he noticed a woman with long blond hair pushing a double stroller, both babies in tiny Santa hats, up the path. She was struggling a bit since there was some snow lodged into the brick joints. For a moment he almost jogged over to push the stroller for her, but something about her reminded him so much of Katie that his legs had turned to lead. She wore big black sunglasses and had a pink wool hat pulled down low so he couldn't see her face, but just something about the way she moved, plus her height and slender figure in the long gray puffy coat, was all Katie Crosby.

The ache spread in his chest at the thought of her, the reminder, and he closed his eyes again and lifted his face to the bright sun. He forced himself to turn away from the woman with the stroller, just like he forced himself not to look at the for-sale signs when he passed them on the way to pack up his grandmother's ranch, which was taking him forever. And now he only had a few weeks.

"Well, I'd better get to the ranch," Asher told his cousins. "I've got *every* room left to go through."

"You need help, we're there," Ford said. "Wives and kids too." His cousins all had small children and a few on the way. Asher loved the little rug rats, lifting them up and flying them overhead to huge giggles. But he wasn't exactly Fun Cousin Ash these days.

"Toddlers are great at packing," Rex said with a grin.

"I've got it, but thanks," Asher said, stepping closer to the tree and lifting the flap of one of the plastic pouches. He pulled out the wish request and tucked it into his pocket. He'd read it later.

As he walked away he could feel his cousins watching him, worrying about him. But he was fine now. Or as fine as he could be. This was the new normal and he'd gotten used to it. Between packing up his grandmother's house, taking care of her beloved goats and his job as a cowboy and wilderness guide at the Dawson Family Guest Ranch, he was busy and distracted.

But he'd never be the same guy he was. A guy who used to love Christmas.

Katie Crosby sat in her car in the town green parking lot, her heart pounding in her chest. She glanced in the rearview mirror at the backs of the twins' rear-facing car seats, wishing she could see their sweet faces right now. Maybe she'd calm down.

She'd seen Asher Dawson in the crowd near the Christmas tree.

Her best friend.

Her former fiancé—however briefly.

The father of her twin baby sons.

The man who thought she was dead.

Asher had been standing with his cousins, her dear friends Ford and Rex Dawson, who'd been her colleagues at the Bear Ridge Police Department, Ford her partner, who'd been training her. When she'd spotted them as she'd been pushing the stroller up one of the little brick pathways, she'd gasped and had been afraid every head would turn to her to see what was wrong, but there was such a crowd by the tree, a group singing "Frosty the Snowman" that the gasp hadn't carried.

She'd only risked stretching her legs and taking the twins out to see the tree because of the huge crowd, never imagining Asher would be there,

that there'd been an event going on. With her long
wavy blond wig, big sunglasses and hat pulled
down low, she'd been unrecognizable. She still
couldn't believe she didn't have to disguise herself anymore. But until she could talk to Asher,
explain everything, she had to be careful.

A few times a day for a year, Katie had read the
news, watched the news, scoured social media accounts for any word about the ex-con who'd threatened to kill everyone she loved, including her "hot
fiancé," Asher Dawson. Katie had been desperate
to see that the woman had been arrested again for
something, anything. But there was always nothing. And Katie had remained in hiding, hours south
of Bear Ridge in a tiny remote town, wearing her
wig, keeping her head down, never getting close
to anyone, except maybe the dear grandmother
next door who babysat the twins while Katie had
worked as a waitress at the diner those first months.

But this morning, the news Katie had been waiting for an entire year, through her pregnancy and
the first three months of her twins' lives, had come.
The ex-con who'd threatened her had been killed
last night during a robbery.

It was over.

Katie, who'd been driving on that mountain
road, in tears over Asher breaking their engagement—the irony adding to her broken heart—had
seen the ex-con behind the wheel of a dark SUV

suddenly behind her, hitting her so hard that she'd lost control of her little car and hit the guardrail before going over the side of the cliff.

My baby, she'd remembered thinking as her car hit the water and sank. Disoriented, panicked, Katie had managed to get out, the current carrying her so fast that she could barely keep her head above water.

She'd been in such despair that she might not have fought so hard to survive had she been alone in that water. But that morning, she'd discovered she was pregnant. She'd gone to Asher's earlier that night to tell him, but before she could get out the words, he'd called off the engagement, the platonic marriage, and she'd been so beside herself that she'd fled. Forgetting for a moment that a vengeful lunatic was out there.

She'd finally found herself clinging to a rock a town over, across the county line, and something about it not being her jurisdiction made her feel a little better about her next move. Which was to get out of the water and find a place to hide out for the night and sleep, her head throbbing. In the morning, when she was still alive and found some soaking wet cash in her pocket, she'd taken a bus out of town and then another that would get her at least three hours away.

In her new town, she'd found word of her presumed death, that her car had been located in the

river, her purse and mittens in the rocky shoreline. The ex-con would be satisfied—and those
Katie loved would be safe. And Katie would wait.
Surely a woman that twisted would be in jail soon
enough and Katie could come home, explain herself.

It had taken until this morning.

Now she had to hope like hell that everyone
would understand—and forgive her.

Particularly Asher.

But what if he'd married someone else and was
now happily a husband, living at his grandmother's ranch? Surely he'd married so he wouldn't
lose the the place. His wife could be pregnant.
Was Katie supposed to burst into his life a year
later with the shocking news that not only was
she alive but that Asher was the father of twin
three-month-old boys?

She closed her eyes for a moment. She'd already made her plan before leaving Thornberry,
the tiny town she'd been hiding out in the past
year. She would drive over to the goat ranch and
park in the stand of trees that would hide her
small car from view, keeping herself down low.
And she would watch, see if there was a woman
around with a gold ring on her hand. She'd look
as hard as she could at Asher's face to see if he
was happy. And she'd know.

Then she'd decide. If she was staying and telling him the truth—all of it. Or if she should just stay hidden. Dead.

That was wrong, though. Terribly wrong.

More wrong than ruining the happiness he might have found this past year.

She couldn't keep the truth from him. Or his children.

That precious man she'd seen standing near the holiday tree, a santa hat over his burnished brown hair, the intense blue eyes, the black leather jacket and the red-and-green scarf she'd knitted him two Christmases ago, was Dylan and Declan's father. The two men beside him, such good, compassionate, dedicated men, were relatives—and Katie had none herself. She was going to deny her sons their family?

If Asher is happily married, and you come knocking on his door, you'll just be complicating his life—not ruining it. She'd always been just his best friend—except for one night when they'd been much more—and he'd never thought of her otherwise. Her return and the babies would be a shock, but then things would settle down. They'd make it work.

She's go on acting like she hadn't been in love with Asher Dawson from the moment she'd met him in kindergarten, a feeling that had never abated. And her babies would have their father. Their uncles and cousins too since there were a slew of Dawsons here in Bear Ridge. They might even have a very nice stepmother, since she knew Asher wouldn't marry just anyone for the inheritance.

She'd looked for a ring on his finger at the tree, but he'd been wearing gloves.

Now, ducked low in her car, she watched Asher head for the parking lot, far enough from where she was parked. She waited until another vehicle pulled behind him on the way out, then slid behind that car. If Asher made a left, he'd be heading for the Dawson Family Guest Ranch where he'd worked as a cowboy and wilderness guide, likely still did. If he made a right, he was going to his grandmother's small ranch, Dawson's Sweet Dairy, where he'd long been the foreman.

He made a right.

She followed at a slow distance since she knew the way by heart.

Fifteen minutes later, she got to the turnoff by a big weeping willow they'd climbed and hidden in as kids. But what was that big sign stuck into the ground?

For Sale.

What?

Why would—

She gasped for the second time that morning. If the estate was selling the ranch, it was because Asher *hadn't* gotten married to fulfill the terms of his grandmother's will—and didn't plan to in the next three weeks by the Christmas deadline. He was letting the ranch go? This place he'd loved since he was born? That didn't make sense. Why hadn't he married someone in the year she'd been gone?

At least there wasn't a wife to contend with. Less complicated.

But she still had to tell the only man she'd ever loved that the past year had been a necessary lie. That she wasn't dead, after all.

And that he had twin baby boys.

Chapter Two

Asher had just finished spreading out fresh hay in the goats' pen in the barn when he heard a car approaching. Could be another Realtor or a drive-by to see the ranch, even someone who'd already had a viewing back for another look. The for-sale signs had gone up a few days ago and he'd made himself scarce for the showings. His Realtor had told him he should really doll the place up for the holidays—at least hang a wreath on the front door if he wasn't going to string lights around the house or the trees or put those single electric candles in the windows.

He wasn't going to do any of that. Like he needed

to be reminded of Christmas when the holiday meant nothing but loss to him?

Besides, he had three offers on the ranch already, two over asking, and was sitting on them. He wanted to get this over with *and* not sign anything at the same time.

Two of the goats, Jelly Bean and Plum Pudding, named by his grandmother, sauntered over looking hopeful about getting a treat. He always had carrot slices in a baggie in his pocket for them. He gave them their snack and a pat each, then left the barn, lowering his hat against the bright sunshine.

He wasn't surprised that offers had come in on Dawson's Sweet Dairy Ranch. The well-kept white farmhouse with its red door and black shutters, surrounded by wood-fenced pastures and distant evergreens, was inviting, and the red barn with its arched white shuttered windows picture-postcard of what a small goat ranch might look like. His grandmother had only sixteen goats at various stages when she'd passed, and Asher had scaled back his hours at his cousins' dude ranch to run this place, then had taken a leave through the new year. He only kept up with the goat milk, which was easy enough for Asher to handle; his grandmother had had a private label and had sold milk and cheese at shops and B and Bs in the county. According to his Realtor, some of those who'd put in offers had no interest in the dairy or breeding business and just wanted the house and land.

His grandmother wouldn't like that one bit. She and his grandfather had bought the property as newlyweds and had raised Asher's father here. There was history, family memories, and Asher had spent every summer here, plus countless days after school and weekends. His father had never had any interest in the ranch, and couldn't stand goats, but his two wives liked Bear Ridge, which had its charms, and so his dad had stayed put, and Asher had been raised in the town since his mother had always stayed too with her subsequent marriages. His mother and her third husband wanted adventure and they were currently on an RV road trip down South, and his father and his fourth wife lived an hour away in a house attached to a healing crystal spa they owned. It was no wonder that Cassie Dawson had left the ranch to Asher—albeit with that stipulation.

Though he had to say he'd been thrown for a loop about that. His grandmother knew that he didn't put much stock in the institution of marriage, not with seven marriages between his parents who were both only in their late fifties. He'd realized right away that his sneaky gram understood that—and also that she'd always wanted him to end up with Katie, to magically fall in love, even though he'd told her for years and years that they were just friends and would always be just friends, that the friendship *mattered*. Cassie Dawson had found a way to get him to propose to Katie, after all. In fact, knowing that was very likely his grandmother's master plan had made him feel all right about going along with it.

But all that had blown up.

Asher stood just outside the barn, expecting his visitor to exit the car any second, but whoever it was just sat there, idling. The Realtors around here all drove fancy SUVs, and this beat-up little black car had definitely seen better days. Maybe it was just someone interested in checking out the property.

He waited but no one got out of the car. There was a woman in the driver's seat. He was a good hundred feet away from where she'd parked but he could see she was staring straight ahead at the pasture.

He gave her another few seconds and then walked over to the car. As he got closer, he realized it was the woman he'd seen with the double stroller at the Christmas tree earlier. The one who'd reminded him of Katie. She was still wearing the big black sunglasses and the hat, her long blond hair tumbling past her shoulders. His appearance by the driver's door didn't make her turn his way. Or move. Or get out.

Who was this?

He rapped on the window. That got her to glance down. Not toward him or at him, but at least there was a sign of movement.

Finally, she looked behind her, then back down, then seemed to be sucking in a breath. The car door opened and she stepped out.

And when she took off her sunglasses, his knees gave out and he dropped to the ground.

He had to be seeing things.

Otherwise, Katie Crosby had just gotten out of that car.

"Asher," she said, dropping to her own knees in front of him. "I have so much to tell you. I'm sorry for the shock."

He stood up, bracing one hand on the car for support, and she bolted up too. That shock had rendered him unable to speak. Or process anything she was saying.

"Katie?" he whispered, reaching out a hand toward her face. She couldn't be real. The stress of Christmas, of the upcoming anniversary of her loss, had clearly gotten to him and he was seeing things. His hand landed on her arm and then he stepped back.

She was real.

Katie was alive?

"I survived the accident," she said, her brown eyes teary. "When I managed to get out of the river, I realized the only way to save the people I loved from the ex-con who'd run me off the road that night was to fake my death. I did it without thinking it through. I found out this morning that we're all finally safe. So I drove up here. With the twins."

He just kept staring at her, trying to process what she was saying.

Managed to get out of the river. Faked her death. With the twins.

What twins?

He slowly shook his head, then looked into the back seat of her car. Two rear-facing car seats.

"You have twins? What?" That didn't make sense.

She sucked in a breath. "*We* have twins, Asher," she whispered. "I'd found out the morning of the accident that I was pregnant. From our one night together. Between the threats and knowing that wasn't what you wanted—a real marriage, let alone children, with me—I made the decision to save those I loved and to let you find someone else. So you could keep this ranch."

"I'm a father?" he said, his gaze once again going to the car seats.

She nodded. "Fraternal twin boys. They're three months old."

Without thinking, he grabbed her into his arms and held her tight, her own arms wrapping around him. He stepped back, staring at her face, then pulled her against him again.

Katie was alive… Katie was alive… Katie was alive. The words echoed in his head, his heart pounding in his chest.

"I'm so sorry about everything, Asher," she said.

Katie Crosby was alive.

He took a step back, trying to catch his breath, to understand. "You could have told me, Katie. You should have told me. You let me think you were dead. I missed the birth of my own children." He shook his head.

This can't be real. Had he stepped on a rake and gotten slammed in the head and knocked himself into a hallucination?

"I was scared out of my mind for you," she said. "And for the pregnancy. I didn't even know that it was twins then. I just kept thinking how I wouldn't be able to hide the pregnancy from that pyscho."

Oh God. "I can't think straight, Katie."

"Let's talk inside the house," she said. She reached into her car and turned off the ignition, then opened the back door and took out one of the car seats. "Will you get the other?"

He stared at her for a second, then down at the baby in the infant carrier. "That's my child," he whispered. He walked around the car and unlatched the other seat, looking down at the sleeping baby. "And you," he said. "You're mine?"

"Their names are Declan and Dylan."

D names, in memory of her late father and his late grandfather. When they were teenagers and would talk about the abstract future, they'd always said they'd choose names beginning with D in honor of Derek Crosby and Dean Dawson. Katie had lost her father at age four. Asher had lost his grandfather when he was fourteen.

As he walked beside her toward the house, he noticed her staring at the for-sale sign.

"So you didn't marry," she asked.

"No," he said and left it at that, aware that she was watching him as he took the steps onto the porch and headed inside, holding the door open for her.

As he closed the door, he looked into the carrier he held. This was his child? He glanced over at the baby asleep in the one Katie held. These were their children. The words echoed in his head, knocking into each other. He needed to sit down.

She put the carrier on the floor beside the coffee table and he did the same, then sat on the sofa, leaning his head back for a moment. "I can't believe any of this. Not computing, Katie. I guess I'm gonna need a minute. Or sixty."

"I understand," she said.

"You barely look like yourself," he said, upping his chin at the long blond hair.

She reached up and took off the wig, stuffing it in her tote bag and then running her hands through the familiar straight brown hair even if it was now past her shoulders. "Feels good to have that thing off. I hated wearing it, but I had to. Easier than keeping up with coloring every six weeks. Particularly with infants to care for."

"Does anyone know you're alive? Besides me?" he asked. "Ford?"

She shook her head. "My plan was to see you first. Then talk to him and then the chief. Apologize."

"If I don't seem overjoyed that you're here, Katie, it's just the shock. Double shock."

"I get it."

The babies began to stir, and Asher stared at them, wondering if he should pick one of them up.

"I'll need to change them and feed them," she said. "If you want to take some time to digest, we can talk once I do that."

He nodded.

She stood up and pulled her tote bag onto her shoulder. "I have everything I need in here. Guest room in the same spot?"

He nodded again and stood.

She took a baby carrier in each hand and walked down the hall.

She'd barely closed the door of the guest room before his legs turned to Jell-O again and he dropped down.

Katie was here. Alive and well.

And he had baby sons.

As Katie sat on the bed in the guest room, the babies both changed and Declan in her arms for his bottle while his twin lay on his play mat on the rug, she closed her eyes, still unable to believe that she was here, that she'd spoken to Asher, told him everything. After a year of waiting, worrying, wondering.

He'd held her. How good that had felt, even if it had been just for a few seconds. And it told her that deep down, no matter what had happened between them that final day, no matter that she'd faked her death, he still cared.

The relief.

She shifted the baby in her arms, letting her gaze wander around the space, so familiar, so dear. How many times had she stayed in this room over the years? Countless. As a kid she'd felt so special being invited to dinner at Asher's grandparents' house, and when offered the chance to spend the night, which meant having her own room, even her own bathroom, she'd felt like a princess. She'd grown up in two different group foster homes, and sharing had been her life. Here, she'd felt part of a family, always included.

She ran a finger down Declan's impossibly smooth cheek. Both babies looked so much like Asher. That had been a comfort the past few months of being so alone, the single mother of twins, unable to reach out to anyone she loved. Unable to share. She'd had nothing when she'd dragged herself out of the water—no purse, no wallet, no photos, no phone. Just some cash and her memories. Some good. Some not.

Like the conversation she and Asher had had before she'd driven off.

Thing was, that night, she'd thought he was saying he'd rather lose the ranch than marry her, that too much had happened between them, that things were strained and awkward because they'd slept together and maybe they could never be the same.

But in an entire year, with the deadline looming to marry in order to inherit Dawson's Sweet Dairy Ranch, he was still single and had put the ranch up for sale. She didn't understand. She knew what this place meant to him. With parents who were multimarried and multidivorced, he'd spent so much time at the ranch. And as Cassie Dawson had gotten on in years, he'd become the foreman so that she could focus on the fun and easy parts of caring for her beloved goats and making her dairy products that were sold all over the county.

She got up and set Declan down on the play mat and picked up his twin, settling back on the bed with Dylan in her arms for his bottle.

There was a knock on the door. She sucked in a breath and called out, "Come on in."

Asher filled the doorway. He stood there for a moment, his gaze on the baby she held. "Can I feed him?"

She smiled, her heart soaring. "Of course."

He sat down next to her and she transferred Dylan into his arms, watching how he carefully held his son, keeping his forearm extra rigid to support his neck, even though he was just past that stage.

"You've had a lot of practice holding your cousins' babies over the past few years," she said. "It shows."

He nodded, staring down at the infant suckling on the bottle. "I can't believe I have two sons. Everything is slowly sinking in, but this," he added, his eyes soft on Dylan. "This is something."

"I know," she said.

He looked up at her, the wariness back. "Tell me everything. You got out of the river and then what?"

"It was late at that point, ten, maybe eleven o'clock. I'm not sure. I'm not sure I was conscious when I first landed. I just know it was dark and there was barely any noise of any cars up above. Just the whooshing of the river."

"I'm sorry I wasn't there for you," he said. "I'm sorry I made you run off like that. And the whole reason you came to see me that night was to tell me you were pregnant?"

She nodded. "I didn't get the chance. You told me the engagement was off and I was so upset I just wanted to get away."

So much had happened between them in such a short period of time—from a year ago last November when his grandmother had died and they'd unexpectedly slept together, to the stipulation in the will, to the marriage proposal and then the take-back the day after Christmas—but all that seemed like ancient history. They had children now. Twin babies. Everything had to be about going forward, not looking back.

She glanced over at Declan on his play mat, his curious gaze on the overhead mobile. "I walked for a while along the riverbank. I was so cold and disoriented and afraid hypothermia would get me in the end. But it wasn't just me I had to take care of—I was very newly pregnant. I came across an empty old fishing cabin and dried off and warmed up best I could. I took a sweatshirt, a pair of jeans and a wool hat I found there and changed into them, and put my wet clothes in a backpack I found. When I took that stuff—stole

that stuff—I knew right then my life as I knew
it was over. That I wasn't a police officer anymore. That the ex-con's threats meant I couldn't
be Katie Crosby anymore."

She didn't add that their argument and the shock
of being run off the cliff had settled into numbness
in her chest along with whatever physical injuries,
however light, she'd sustained from the crash. She
hadn't been herself that night. She'd only known
she couldn't go back to Bear Ridge and put everyone she loved in danger. Including the baby she
hadn't yet known was twins.

She watched him shift Dylan up a bit and continue feeding him as if it was natural.

"I could only imagine what a panic you were
in, Katie," he said. "Don't beat yourself up about
taking some old clothes and a backpack. You
gave to the community and county plenty over
the years. And in that cabin, *you* needed."

"I appreciate you saying that. Taking what
wasn't mine stuck with me awhile."

He glanced up at her and nodded thoughtfully.
"So you left the cabin and went where?"

"I took a bus as far as half my money would
take me, bought a box of hair dye in a convenience store and spent my last thirty bucks on
a very cheap motel room where I slept hard. In
the morning I walked into the next town, a small
ranching community called Thornberry with a

bunch of basic shops like a diner and a convenience store and a gas station. There was a help-wanted sign in the diner and I got the job and found out about an old-timey boardinghouse within walking distance. That was all I needed."

"Was the town welcoming?" he asked.

"Not really at first. I made up a story about traveling the state. But Thornberry is the kind of place where people don't ask a lot of questions. It was perfect for me. The first full day there, I saw a bit about myself on the evening news on the TV at the diner. A Bear Ridge rookie police officer presumed dead in a car accident off Cliffside Road."

He winced and she instinctively put her hand on his arm, the feel of him under her fingers almost electrified, thrumming.

"The pregnancy kept me going. Once I got my first paycheck I could afford the local clinic and prenatal vitamins and I found out I was having twins. I wanted to call you so many times, Asher. But I knew you'd drive right down and try to convince me to come home when I couldn't. Not with that maniac out there."

He didn't respond and she wasn't sure he understood or not. Maybe he did intellectually, but she could see from his expression, from how rigid he still held himself, that he didn't understand *emotionally*.

"I guess you felt disconnected from me as it was," he finally said. "After I ended the engagement."

"Yeah," she whispered.

Dylan was done with his bottle. Asher held him vertically against his chest and gave his back a gentle pat until the baby burped.

"I'll say a proper hello to Declan now," he said, going over to the play mat and picking up the little guy. Declan stared at him, his father, his big blue eyes so focused.

"They look a lot like me," Asher said, wonder in his voice.

"They do," she agreed.

He set Declan back down on the mat. "Why don't I go make us something to eat," he said, standing up.

"Sounds good."

She missed him the moment he left the room.

Chapter Three

Asher felt so unsettled as he rooted around his fridge and cabinets for what to make for dinner. Something ordinary like he'd make any old night seemed wrong. This was a special occasion; Katie was back.

And he had *children*.

If he kept repeating that, maybe it would sink in, feel real. But right now, nothing about this situation felt real.

He hated to say it, but Katie seemed like a stranger.

Because of the year that had gone by? The choices she'd had to make? The separation? The year of grief? Where they'd stood before she'd fled in her car?

All of the above.

He'd have to give it time. So would she.

The moment she appeared in the doorway of the kitchen, a baby carrier in each arm, he knew one thing: he wanted her to stay here with him, with the babies.

"We need to get to know each other all over again," he said. "These new people we are. I know I'm not the same guy I was a year ago. And I'm sure you're not the same woman."

"Not a bit," she said. She set down the carriers beside the door, stuffing her hands into the pockets of her jeans.

"And I want to get to know my sons. I'd like them to stay here. For all of you to stay here. I only have the place till Christmas and I like the idea of being here with them. At least they'll have a little bit of their legacy." He leaned against the counter, crossing his arms over his chest, wondering what she'd say.

"I was so sure you'd married," she said. "I was prepared to see a wife with the goats in the pasture or in the barn. It never occurred to me once all year that you'd let the ranch go."

"I messed up with you, Katie—our last conversation, particularly. At the time it felt right but after I thought I lost you, I was a wreck, as you can imagine. I associated marriage with you, the ranch with you. And there was no way I'd dishonor your memory by marrying another woman just to keep the place. It would have felt like a dishonor to my grandmother too."

"Because she always hoped we'd get married."

He nodded. "What's funny is she'd always tell me not to get too wrapped up in being 'in love,' that it was love-love that kept a marriage strong and going. But then she'd shake her head and say that of course I should be in love and add an 'oh, what the hell do I know?'"

Katie smiled. "She knew a lot. I always thought she was the wisest, kindest person."

He nodded. "Me too." He looked at the babies. "So what do three-month-olds do?"

"More than you'd think. They've discovered their fists and like to gnaw on their hands. They have huge laughs. They like staring at each other and other people. Their gazes just fix on someone and it's so funny."

"Do you have any of their things? If not, we can go shopping in the morning and pick up whatever they need."

"I've only ever had the basics and some thrift-store finds that served me really well," she said. "I brought the stuff they really need. I have their folding bassinets in the trunk."

"Once I get dinner on, I'll go bring everything in. Pasta sound good?"

"My favorite comfort food," she said. "Need help?"

"I've got it."

She nodded, then said, "I'll take them into the living room and put them on the rug for some tummy time. They like being on their bellies and lifting their heads. They're just starting to turn their heads. The milestones are really coming these days."

He looked at his sons, the faces so like his own, the blue eyes, the brown hair. "I'm sorry I missed any of it. But I'm glad it was only the first three months. I almost feel lucky it wasn't longer."

"I know what you mean," she said with a gentle smile, and he was struck by the urge to hold her again, to let her know everything was okay now, they'd figure things out. They were still Asher and Katie, friends since age five, even if they felt like awkward strangers right now. That would pass, surely.

She picked up the carriers and went into the living room and he sucked in a breath and then grabbed what he needed from the fridge. The prosciutto. Peas. Parmesan. Four eggs. Olive oil. The box of linguini.

He set the water to boil and got out the sauté pan, then he went outside to bring in the contents of the trunk. Katie's car had definitely seen bet-ter days. It had to be fifteen years old with its share of dings and he wasn't sure he'd trust it to even get to town, despite the snow tires he was glad to see.

In the trunk were the bassinets, three duffel bags and a plastic tub that he finally realized was a baby bath. He made three trips to carry every-thing in. Katie was sitting cross-legged on the rug in front of the twins, who were lifting their heads like turtles. He watched them for a moment, then brought the bassinets and the bags into the guest room before stopping in the arched doorway of the living room.

"You could take my grandmother's room," he said. "It's basically been turned into another guest room. The Realtor had me stage it to appeal to people by basically taking the grandmotherliness out of it. And the guest room can be the nursery. Or they can stay with you. Or me. Whatever you think."

"Actually, having them in their own room sounds wonderful," she said. "They've never had a nurs-ery before."

"After dinner I'll take the bed out to give them more room and tomorrow we can pick up what-ever else they might need. Or what you might want for them."

"Sounds good. I'll go show them their room

and get it set up. They'll be ready for bed in a couple of hours. You'll be glad to know they're just starting to make it a good six hours without waking up."

"I'm fine with being woken up by my own babies in the middle of the night," he said. "I'm strangely looking forward to it."

She smiled, then gave the air a sniff. "Whatever you're making smells delicious."

"Linguini Carbonara. You always used to love it, and I have all the ingredients. A good Italian bread too."

"Can't wait," she said, then put both boys in their carriers, gave him another smile and headed into the guest room.

She was gone for a good twenty minutes. He'd just poured the linguini into the pan of sauce and prosciutto and peas when she came back, a carrier in each hand. He had a feeling she'd needed a little time behind closed doors to digest everything he'd said—the offer to stay in particular. At this point, it wasn't like she could go anywhere else, tonight at least.

She'd changed her clothes too. She wore faded blue jeans that molded to her tall, slender body and a long fuzzy cardigan over a tank top. Her silky brown hair was in a low ponytail. Her pink-red lips were slightly glistening and smelled faintly of cherries—her favorite lip balm, he knew. He'd missed the sight of her so much that he drank in every bit of her. The warm light brown eyes with the long lashes. The bit of freckles across her nose. Her collarbone. He wasn't sure he'd ever noticed that before.

He swallowed and shifted his attention back to the pan of pasta, giving it an unnecessary stir just to have something to do.

She set the carriers on the edge of the rug between the table and the window, playing a few rounds of peekaboo. There were now two mobiles attached to the carriers, and the twins seemed taken by the lightly spinning circles and squares in pastel colors and different textures.

He pictured her in hiding, handling everything herself. She'd likely just gotten by, spending her paycheck on whatever the babies needed. As he sliced the Italian bread and put it in a basket, he wondered if she'd made friends, or if she hadn't allowed herself, given that she was hiding. It must have been a very lonely time. Even with the babies for company. She'd been all they had—no father, no family. No one.

"Did you leave anyone behind you'll miss?" he asked and then froze. He hadn't meant to ask like that, as though he was talking about a boyfriend. "You don't have to answer that. I don't mean to pry." But he did wonder. And want to know. Not that it was any of his business. The idea of another man touching her, kissing her, waiting for her, had his chest twitching.

That was also unusual. He'd never felt a stir of jealousy over guys Katie had dated before. Maybe now, the difference was the twins. Someone else stepping in as a father figure these past three months.

You should be grateful to anyone who helped her, who was kind and good to her and to the twins, he reminded himself. He turned away for a second, not sure what the hell was going on in his head.

She sat at the table and took a sip of the iced tea he'd set out. Katie loved peach iced tea, sweet and cold. "No," she finally said. "I had to lay low. I couldn't imagine meeting someone and having to lie to him about who I really was. And then there was the matter of being pregnant and not yet showing. I'd have to disclose that on a first date and how awkward would that be? 'Oh, by the way, I'm pregnant with another man's baby.'"

Mine, he thought, picking up the platter of pasta to bring over to the table. "I wish I could have been there for you, Katie. I hate the thought of you so alone in the middle of nowhere. No one to turn to." He put the platter on the table with a shake of his head, his gaze moving from her to the twins and back to Katie again.

"If it helps, I did have a pretty good setup.

I'd lost my job at the diner because the owner's daughter needed work and they didn't need a third waitress, but I found a good thing at a nearby ranch as a hand. The job came with a cabin. I'd just started showing when I interviewed so it was clear I was pregnant. I think the ranch owners— a married couple—felt sorry for me since it was clear I was alone and not saying much. They were kind but I was careful not to get close. I worked part-time, mindful how physical the job was. Afterward, the wife's mother babysat for me for peanuts while I worked."

"I'm relieved you had a good safe place to live and keep your head above water," he said, sitting across from her.

"Thanks to your grandmother, I made myself indispensable since I knew so much about taking care of goats. They'd lost their goat hand, so we both got something we needed. I started to feel at home there and then it wasn't so lonely. Between the babies and the goats, I had good company."

He took a bite of pasta. "Well, once you've talked to the chief and everyone discovers that you're alive and back, do you think you'll want to rejoin the PD?"

"I can't see it, honestly. Or at least not right away. I wouldn't want to leave the twins for a full-time stretch and I've been out of the game an entire year. I'm not sure what became of my bank account or my apartment and everything in it given that I was presumed dead. I guess I'll find out all that tomorrow. I'd be happy to help out with the goats until—"

Until Christmas. When I have to sell this place.

He felt that familiar ache burrow into his chest at the thought of having to give up Dawson's Sweet Dairy Ranch. He might have accepted it, but he was far from making peace with it. "Because you had a will that left everything to me, I was the one they called to sort through your things. Your bank account was frozen because you couldn't yet be declared dead. I have all your things upstairs in the attic, and your furniture's in storage."

"Wow," she said. "That's good to know. That I won't be starting from scratch all over again. And thanks for all this," she said, heaping pasta on her plate. "Smells amazing." But she wasn't smiling or looking at him. In fact she looked like she might cry. "I can't believe you have to give this place up."

He reached out to cover her hand with his own. "You got through a year on your own in hiding—with newborn twins, Katie Crosby. I can get through having to sell the ranch."

That didn't seem to make her feel better. She pushed around pasta on her plate, and he hoped she hadn't lost her appetite.

As he moved his hand away, he wanted to hug her again. Just stand there and hold her.

He looked down at the twins in their baby seats. Dylan yawned and Declan was rubbing at his eyes. These were his sons—*his* sons. That he was a father still didn't feel real.

He looked at Katie, who was now holding a piece of Italian bread without seeming to have any intention of taking a bite.

She was freshly back from a rough year on her own.

He had a family ranch—that she'd always been a big part of—that he was about to lose.

A family ranch that he suddenly had all the more reason to keep—*and* keep in the family. For his twins. He wanted his boys with him so he wouldn't miss another minute of their lives. He wanted to give Katie a home and security. He wanted to give her back something of what she'd lost.

Her best friend.

Maybe he could propose marriage all over again. He'd keep the ranch. They'd raise their children here together. They didn't have to talk about how the marriage would work or what they would be to each other. Right now, they both just needed a soft place to land.

And that soft place wasn't just the ranch—but each other.

Sleep on it, he told himself. *Don't blurt out a proposal. Think it through. From both your vantage points.*

But there was another thing different this time around.

His awareness of her. As a woman. One he knew so well and didn't know at all anymore.

Katie lay in her bed in the big bedroom that had been Cassie Dawson's, alternating between staring up at the ceiling and out the windows at the dark night. Then every five seconds her gaze would shoot to where she expected the twins' bassinets to be, but they were in the nursery next door. That would take some getting used to.

The room was nice, all soothing pale gray walls and white trim, a very fluffy muted duvet with a down comforter inside and four soft pillows. She recognized the dresser with its big round mirror. Katie remembered the dresser top holding all kinds of perfumes and lotions with tangles of costume jewelry. She'd loved the room the way it had been, lace doilies and tapestries hung on the wall, but if she knew one thing, it was that very little stayed the same.

Except for her feelings for Asher, it seemed.

But everything was different between them now. They were so tentative around each other, walking on eggshells, unsure how they fit now.

If they fit. They'd always been so comfortable around each other, could finish each other's sentences to the point that they fully understood each other without saying a word. He'd known her deepest fears, her biggest secrets, her greatest hopes. And she'd known his. But now, all that had changed too. Her hopes centered around the twins and a fresh start here in Bear Ridge, if that was possible. And Asher had been through so much the past year that what drove him—or didn't—was beyond her. She didn't really know him anymore.

She stared up at the ceiling again, one thought knocking around her head, her heart.

She'd marry him to save the ranch. He had to know that, and he hadn't brought it up.

Even now, when they had all the more reason to join forces. For the twins.

She wasn't going to mention it, though. This was his business.

But she couldn't help wondering if he wouldn't propose to keep the ranch because of all that had happened last year. Water under the ole bridge. Nothing in their past could count anymore, hold much weight. Only now mattered. The twins. Being parents.

And the fact that he had three weeks to marry someone, anyone, or sell the place.

She couldn't imagine him letting that happen.

She loved Dawson's Sweet Dairy Ranch so much and she couldn't come close to feeling about it the way Asher did. Or then again, maybe she could. It had been a sanctuary for both of them when they had nowhere else to go. Katie to her foster home. Asher to two empty houses since his divorced parents were rarely home by the time he was a teen.

Once, she and Asher were exploring in the attic, and Katie had found all these brochures about becoming a foster parent. She'd gasped, wondering if Cassie Dawson had been thinking about taking her in. But in that same big file, she'd found a letter attached to a county brochure, a copy she assumed, that Cassie had written to the state agency. She'd recently lost her husband and was in poor health and didn't think she could do right by Katie but she'd welcome her into her home anytime for visits and be a grandmotherly figure. She'd burst into tears and so Asher had come over and seen the letter before she could put it away. Katie wasn't sure it was something his grandmother had wanted him to know.

You were this close to being my sister, he'd said in that way he had of diffusing a very emotional moment. *But you already feel like that anyway*, he'd added.

She could remember thinking: *I can't say the same about you, buddy.*

Asher Dawson had never felt like a brother, not that she'd ever had one. Being madly in love, forever, with the guy had made sure of that. Possessive of him in elementary school when other girls had crushes. Full-out in love by middle school. Hopelessly devoted in high school but by then she was used to watching him with his girlfriends, the prettiest girls in town with amazing bodies and hair that flipped just so. Hers had always just lain there, boring brown. Katie and her freckles. Katie and her stick-straight body without a curve in sight. No matter what, though, Asher had been there for her, her loyal best friend. She'd had a bad night at the prom with her date, who'd been very handsy and secretly drinking, and Asher had spent a good amount of time with her, telling off the guy, making sure the teacher chaperones knew the kid shouldn't be driving, and then Asher took her home, infuriating his girlfriend, who'd dumped him in the parking lot.

Had she and Asher magically gotten together that night? Had he finally seen her as a young woman, and not his buddy of many years?

Nope. She thought about all the dates and short-term relationships she'd had, trying to find her Mr. Right, trying not to compare everyone to Asher Dawson. But when you felt so much about someone, how could you just block it out? When your heart was consumed by someone else, even by someone who didn't return those feelings, how did you just stop? She really had tried, though. She'd kept an open mind. But in the end, no one lasted. No one had been Asher. Or had come close. No one had captured her heart the way he had.

And the man still had it.

More so now that they shared such a powerful connection: the twins.

A cry sounded just then as if on cue. She gave it fifteen seconds, since the boys had been able to soothe themselves back to sleep sometimes if she didn't go running over and pick up the crier. But no, another cry came and then a longer one. Katie got up and headed in the hallway, not wanting Asher to get woken up at 2:00 a.m., but she realized the cries had stopped. And Asher probably wasn't sleeping either. In fact, she suspected he'd been doing just what she was: staring up at the ceiling. Thinking.

She went into the nursery to check on the twins; she was pretty sure the cries had been Declan, but sometimes she got that wrong. She gasped when she saw Asher sitting on the wooden rocker by the window with Declan in his arms, holding him against his chest and gently rubbing the back of his fleece pj's.

Asher wore a black T-shirt and gray Wyoming Cowboys sweats that he'd had forever. His feet were bare, like hers. "I've got it," he said. "He quieted down right away."

She smiled, her heart going five times bigger at the way he tenderly looked at the baby. His son.

"I checked his diaper," he said. "Dry."

"Wow, you hit the ground running at fatherhood, Asher. I'm impressed."

"Like I said, I've got three months to make up for." He looked down at Declan, the baby's eyes drooping, then up at her. "Tell me everything, Katie. Start with labor pains and go from there. I want to know every detail of their lives."

She wanted to laugh and cry at the same time. Katie sat down on the desk chair. "I went into labor on the most beautiful September morning—September 4. The sky was so blue with such fluffy white clouds. I'd been outside, giving a couple of the goats some treats, when my water broke, and my boss happened to be nearby and got me to the hospital with my go bag. She'd had to come back to the ranch, but her mom stayed with me the whole time. Seven hours of labor. They were born that afternoon, just past three o'clock."

"I'm glad you weren't alone," he said.

"Me too. A girlfriend I'd made at the diner and a bunch of the ranch hands came by with gifts for the babies I almost cried I was so surprised. But people will do that—surprise you with how wonderful they can be. I was scared to be on my own and in hiding and so unsure of everything and missing Bear Ridge so much, but having that community helped me feel less alone."

"I'm really relieved to hear it," he said, gently caressing Declan's head. The baby was asleep.

"They were both six pounds, two ounces. Twenty inches long. Declan was first, then Dylan came a minute and a half later. They were easy babies from the start. They did their share of crying, don't get me wrong, but overall, easy babies. Not too fussy, eat well, burp easily. No major illnesses. They love their naps."

"What are they like? Their personalities?"

"I might be totally wrong," she said. "But I think Declan is the more serious one. Dylan seems more easygoing, always giggling."

He smiled down at his son. "They're lucky to have each other."

Katie had always wanted a sister. A few of her foster sisters over the years had felt like family to her but she'd lost contact with them during moves, hers or theirs. Once, when she was seven, her mother had come to visit her at the home during Christmas even though she didn't have visitation rights because of her drug use. Katie had told her that her friend Beth felt like a real sister, and her mother had said: *I'm your only real family and don't you forget it.*

Katie had tried to forget it, but she'd never been able to.

Her mother had no idea she was a grandmother. Katie sighed, as always wishing things could have been different between them. But Katie had been estranged from her mother for years now. She had no idea where the woman was. Her mother was a drug addict and something of a desperate con artist and lived under aliases to avoid her probation officers. Katie wasn't sure if she was even still in Wyoming.

Once Katie had become a mother, she couldn't imagine the life Celia Crosby had chosen over her own daughter, stuck in foster care when her father had died when Katie was four. But her mother was an addict, and that wasn't a choice, hard as it was for Katie to accept.

"Declan loves his teething toys," Katie said fast to stop the barrage of memories that always followed when she thought of her mom. "His favorite is that chewable little book on the dresser. And Dylan loves the color orange. You can just hold an orange hat in front of him and he'll start laughing hysterically. His eyes light up when I put him in orange. So he's usually wearing orange."

"I have so much to learn about you and your brother," he said softly, reverently to Declan, his gaze so tender on the baby that Katie inwardly sighed.

"Will he go into the bassinet without waking?" he asked. "I'd be fine holding him all night just like this, but then I'd feel like I'd have to scoop up Dylan for dad time too and I'd hate to wake him up by accident."

Awww. "He should go in easily. He's definitely sound asleep."

He carefully stood up and walked over to the bassinet that stood right by Dylan's. He gently put the baby down. Not a peep. Declan lifted a little fist up by his head, his bow lips giving a quirk.

"They're so beautiful," Asher whispered. "I can't believe they're mine."

Well, you're beautiful, she almost said, but didn't.

The way the moonlight just lit up his tousled brown hair, the emotion in his eyes, in his voice. She wished she could fling herself in his arms.

"I'm so glad you're here, Katie," he said, holding her gaze.

"Me too." She also wished she could read his mind—for real. There was such depth of emotion in his voice, such reverence. But was there something else? Something romantic in his expression, his intense blue eyes, the way he looked at her? Maybe just her wishful thinking. In any case, the tension she felt in the air was too much.

She swallowed and darted over to the bassinets, looking at their boys, and as usual, just the sight of them, her focus on them had her head back on straight. "They don't have birth certificates," she said suddenly, that pit forming in her stomach whenever she thought about that fact. "I couldn't imagine filling out the forms with my fake name. Sara Fielding."

"We'll get that taken care of tomorrow," he said, giving her hand a squeeze. "You did the best you could, Katie. No worries."

And then she did fly into his arms. She sensed his momentary hesitation, but just momentary, and then he wrapped those strong, comforting arms around her and held her.

"Everything will be okay," he said.

She looked up at him and smiled. "That was always your mantra to me. And it always made me feel better."

He ran a hand down a tendril of her hair, an affectionate move he'd made countless times over the years, then stepped back, his arms falling to his sides. "Well, I'll let you get back to sleep."

But she could have stayed in that room with him all night. Or better yet, curled up beside him in his bed. Just talking about everything and nothing. Just being together.

Once again, when he left, all she wanted was

to follow him. Go where he went. Be wherever he was.

Like old times. But she and Asher were now *nothing* like old times.

Chapter Four

Asher's alarm buzzed at 5:00 a.m., and he was surprised the house was quiet even that early. He knew from his cousins that babies sometimes started their day well before dawn, which was early even for a rancher. He was already a bit bleary-eyed from the middle-of-the night waking but he'd loved every minute of that time with Declan. And then Katie. It had taken him a good hour to fall asleep after that.

He stayed in bed for a little while, waiting to hear that first cry—his children's—but the house was silent. Maybe Katie and the twins had gotten up and were downstairs and he was the late one? He slid out of bed and took a fast shower, not wanting to miss any time with his sons. Or Katie. Last night, when he'd been in bed, before he'd heard one of the babies cry, he'd had such a powerful urge to be with them. She was the mother of his children; he supposed that was why he was having such a strong and different kind of reaction to her. Everything was different now. He poked his head into the hallway. Silence. In the nursery he saw that the twins were still asleep.

He went downstairs and, though Katie wasn't around, she'd made a pot of coffee. He glanced out the window toward the barn and saw her talking to the goats in the pasture, giving Ellie-Belly a pat on her cinnamon-splotched white nose, a mug of coffee in her hand. He watched her look around and sip her coffee as if bracing herself for what lay ahead this morning: revealing herself to the Bear Ridge Police Department and explaining what had happened.

When she came in, her cheeks red from the cold, Asher called out a hello and she appeared in the doorway, her gloved hands wrapped around the mug. "Morning," she said.

He smiled and poured himself coffee. "Thanks for making this."

"Of course. I was just in the barn. I let the goats out of their pen and gave them fresh hay in the slats and filled up their water pans. The kids are adorable. What are their names?"

"Fritz and Lulu," he said. "No idea why I named them that. I just looked at them when they were born and they were Fritz and Lulu."

She grinned and topped off her coffee. "I got to name one of the kids last spring at the ranch I worked at and the name just came to me out of the blue in the same way. Penny Lane." She glanced out the window at the goats, two of which were still in the warmer enclosure in the barn. Lizzie and Violet liked to snuggle in the hay but the other four preferred to be outside even in cold snaps, jumping on their favorite logs.

Katie leaned against the counter and took a sip of coffee. She gestured at the baby monitor on the table. "The twins were still fast asleep when I went out five minutes ago and not a peep since."

"My cousins will be jealous," he said. "Daisy's newborn wakes up every ten minutes apparently."

"Been there," she said with a playful frown. "They've been sleeping later and later this month. We got past four thirty. But that was my wake-up time anyway at the ranch."

"Ranches and babies are definitely compatible. Even when there are roosters around."

He loved seeing her smile. Her face had been so strained yesterday, but she seemed more comfortable this morning. They'd gotten through yesterday. And their first night.

"So I was thinking about how to suddenly reveal to the chief and my former colleagues that I'm alive and well," she said. "Tell me what you think. We'll drive down to the station, me in disguise, and you can call Ford from the parking lot and tell him that you need to see him and the chief and that's it urgent and ask them to come meet you in the lot. We can talk in your truck so there's full privacy."

"That sounds good to me. While you three talk, I'll put the babies in their stroller and walk them around a bit."

She nodded. "I hope Chief Harringer understands. And Ford. And Gigi. I'm so worried how they'll react."

Gigi Robertson had been a rookie on the force with Katie, and they'd been close friends. She was now partnered with Rex, Asher's other cousin who used to be a US marshal.

"I can't imagine they won't understand why you did what you did," he said. "I certainly understand. I don't like it, but given the position you were in, the pregnancy, I get why you went that route. I think they'll understand too."

Relief crossed her face. "I hope so."

The first cry sounded from upstairs, then another. "I'll get them," he said.

"And I'll make breakfast?" she asked.

"Sounds good. I'm up for anything you find. I do have a craving for eggs over easy."

She smiled. "You always did."

"See, some things never change."

"Hoping so," she said. "And not."

There was a lot she could mean by *and not*, but one of the twins was fussing up a storm, so Asher took the stairs two at a time. But it reminded him that they weren't the same duo they'd been for twenty-five years, that everything was different now. Not just their dynamic, but each of them, as well. That left him feeling unsettled, but as he entered the nursery, the sight of his little babies made him burst into a smile, absolute wonder filling his head and his heart. He was a father now, and that would always come first.

A half hour after meeting with the chief and Ford, first in Asher's truck and then in the chief's office, Katie and Gigi sat at the round table by the window in the women's locker room at the Bear Ridge Police Station, each with a mug of coffee and half of the last doughnut they'd found in the bakery box at the coffee station. The big reveal had gone well, exactly as Katie had hoped, with the chief and Ford, her former partner and trainer, fully understanding her position. Chief Harringer even insisted on throwing her something of a welcome home party and inviting the town and had then gone to call an emergency staff meeting to let them know about Katie while she waited in his office. Katie knew the meeting had gone well because Gigi, in her blue uniform, blond ponytail flying, had come racing into the chief's office, took one look at her and burst into tears as she threw her arms around her old friend.

Once the initial meeting had ended, Asher had taken the twins over to his cousin Daisy's house at the Dawson Family Guest Ranch. She'd have a half hour to meet with Gigi, and then Asher would come pick her up and they'd head into Brewster, the bigger town next door, to go shopping for what the twins needed.

"I still can't believe I'm sitting here with you," Gigi said, her hazel eyes filling with tears again. She reached across the table to grab Katie's hands in hers, her diamond engagement ring twinkling. Gigi and her fiancé had recently gotten engaged after a year together. Last December, before… everything, Katie remembered how excited her friend was about the new guy she'd met at an advanced training seminar they'd all attended for rookies. Her fiancé was a cop with the force in Brewster. "I'm so happy you're here. And I think you and Asher are exactly where you're supposed to be right now. I have a feeling things are going to move slowly and then very fast."

Over the past half hour, Katie had told Gigi everything. She was the only one who knew—at the time and even now, Katie was pretty sure—that Asher's marriage proposal two Novembers ago was because of the stipulation in Cassie Dawson's will. She'd also told her friend about her and Asher's very unexpected night together and how he'd woken up in the middle of the night with regret all over his face. According to Gigi, that they'd ended up in bed together meant that Asher had very deep, very real unacknowledged romantic feelings for her. His lowered inhibitions from a few drinks had simply brought those feelings to the surface. Then once he woke up sober, the wall he'd erected between them in the supposed name of "preserving the friendship" had rebuilt itself.

Katie liked every word that had come out of Gigi's mouth. But she had no idea if any of it was true. *Could* Asher have buried romantic feelings? Was he really so afraid of losing her to the ups and downs of a romance that he'd kept their relationship strictly friendship based? He'd said that was the reason he was ending the engagement—and not to tie her down for a year.

Gigi had thought Asher's distance after they'd slept together was also proof. Otherwise he would have brushed off their night together to alcohol and stress and it wouldn't have gotten him so turned around.

Maybe. Maybe not.

But Asher was also a man of integrity, and she knew then as she knew now that sex—even one night—wasn't something he'd take lightly.

In any case, last year, Gigi had been as hopeful as Katie that once they were married, platonically and not sharing a bedroom, that things would change, and he'd suddenly see his wife as…his wife and not just his bestie since they were five years old.

But not even Gigi had known that Asher had been so torn apart that he'd rescinded the marriage proposal the day after Christmas. Or that Katie had just found out she was pregnant hours earlier.

"You must have been so heartbroken," Gigi said, shaking her head. "I feel so terrible to think of you sobbing your heart out, newly pregnant, trying to get home, and that psychotic stalker comes out of nowhere and rams you off the side of the cliff. Given everything—the crash, your fear and how absolute Asher sounded—it really makes sense why you felt you had to fake your death. The stalker had designs on everyone you cared about. I think what you did was selfless, Katie."

Katie squeezed her friend's hand. "I appreciate that so much, Gigi."

They both sipped their coffees, Katie popping a piece of strawberry frosted doughnut in her mouth.

"No way will he let the ranch go now that you're back," Gigi said. "The man has a chance to undo his mistake."

Katie wasn't so sure he saw it that way. "Last night, the subject of the ranch and having to sell it came up, and I almost asked him to marry me right then and there. But he'd made it clear last year that he thinks that's a terrible idea. So I just kept my mouth shut."

"Well, when he ended the engagement, he didn't know you were pregnant. Now the two of you have twins together. If that and saving the ranch aren't reason enough for you to get married…"

"Except now I know there's no chance of him seeing me as anything other than his plain-Jane best friend with freckles and a boy's body."

Katie guffawed. "Hello, have you seen your boobs now that you're a mother? Pregnancy and childbirth have turned you into Jessica Rabbit."

Katie laughed. "Hardly. But I don't think it was my lack of makeup and curves that kept Asher from seeing me as a woman, Gigi. He was just never interested in me that way. I was his bestie, and that really mattered to him. He watched his parents marry and divorce three or four times and every time he got close to one of their significant others or spouses, there'd be a replacement. Constancy means a lot to him."

"All the more reason to marry the mother of his children and see what happens. The two of you aren't the same people you were last December. In so many ways, both of you have changed. I don't think you can take anything that happened last year as a sign of what's to come now."

Katie was afraid to admit how much she hoped her friend was right.

"I have a question for you," Gigi said, a shy smile on her face. "Will you be my maid of honor?"

Katie gasped and leaped up and grabbed her friend into a hug. "I would love that. You have no idea how much it means to me that you asked. I was so afraid you'd be angry with me for what I did or not reaching out."

"No way," Gigi said. "And it's going to be fun planning our weddings together."

Katie raised an eyebrow. "First of all, *I'm* not engaged. Second of all, if he *does* ask me—for the reasons you mentioned—I doubt we'll be planning a dream wedding, Geej. It would probably just be a quick ceremony at the town hall to make it legal so that he can submit the paperwork to his grandmother's attorney."

"Well, I'll wait to hear that you're engaged, which I'm sure will be happening by tonight. And then we'll plan your wedding. Even if it is at the town hall and there's no bridal party, you'll need a dress and shoes and a bouquet and your hair and makeup done."

Katie grinned. "I'll take you up on all that."

Would Asher propose marriage? For the two big reasons—because they were now parents of baby twins and to save the ranch? With every bit of her heart, she hoped so. She wanted him to have the ranch. She wanted it to stay in the family for the boys.

And she wanted to marry Asher Dawson and have a chance of turning his head. Making him see her differently. Making him want her. Things did change; they were both proof of that.

And if he didn't propose? If he'd rather lose his beloved goat ranch than marry his best friend? The mother of his twin babies?

All because their one night together had made things awkward for a short time and because she might have made it clear that she had feelings for him. Big feelings.

When she'd emphasized the part about how *he'd* regretted that they'd slept together.

He'd ended their engagement to protect her; he'd said that, not in so many words, but she understood that to be true. Because back then, she'd understood him. So well.

Now things were different.

If Christmas closed in without them getting married, she'd…well, she'd cross that bridge when it was about to crumble into the Bear Ridge River.

Chapter Five

Once his cousin Daisy—the lone female sibling among her five brothers and other Dawson cousins—learned that Asher was the father of twin three-month-old boys, she'd texted her brothers and their wives and suddenly the family room at the main house at the Dawson Family Guest Ranch was overrun by Dawsons and little tykes. Ford and Rex were at work at the police station, but his cousin Noah and his wife, Sara, manager and forewoman of the dude ranch, parents of toddler twins and a baby, stopped by, along with Maisey, Rex's wife, and their toddler.

Asher liked how close the cousins were—particularly the twins. They sought each other out.

"Should we get another cookie?" little Chase had asked his twin.

"Do you think we should?" Annabel had responded with huge blue serious eyes.

"I think we should," was his answer and they giggled and ran to the big coffee table, which Daisy had heaped with desserts and pitchers of various beverages.

"Wow, wow, wow," Maisey said when she'd heard the whole story. "What a relief that that despicable stalker didn't steal more time from the three of you becoming the family you are."

Whoa. Wait just a minute. Family? He hadn't thought of them that way.

You are family, though. You're the twins' father. Katie is their mother. You're family even if you and Katie aren't...a couple. That's why you should get married.

But then what? he wondered. He and Katie would have a platonic marriage forever? For eighteen years? Then magically divorce and find their supposed soul mates?

He was missing something here, something he couldn't put his finger on. He had parts of the equation, but he was coming up blank on the answer.

If real marriage doesn't last, like your parents' multiple trips down the aisle, then you should be rushing to propose. So that you and Katie can

*raise the twins together in the family home, the
family ranch. You both love that place. It makes
sense.*

Last November, when he'd proposed the first
time around, he'd been envisioning the two of
them staying married to adhere to the terms of
the will. They'd marry by Christmas of this year
and stay married for one year, per the will, then
they could go their separate ways. But who was
going a separate way with twin babies?

How many times was he going to think the
same thing: *Everything is different now.*

"The two of you must have a lot to work out,"
Daisy said, Declan in her arms while he held
Dylan. "You'll all come to our big Christmas
party the Friday night before Christmas, right?
Everyone will get to meet their new cousins."

"We'll definitely come," he said.

With a possibility of attending the family party
as a married couple with children.

Boy, had his life changed fast.

"I had such a great time with Gigi," Katie said
as Asher drove them to BabyLand a big baby
store in the next town, the twins in their rear-facing car seats. "It felt so good to be myself with a
friend. The real me, my name, no disguise, talking about the truth. It's like Katie Crosby really
has come back to life."

"Best day of my life," he said, then felt his cheeks heat up a little. He hadn't meant to say that even though it come barreling into his head.

"That's really a sweet thing to say, Asher." She was looking at him and then she put her hand on his arm and he almost swerved a bit.

How many times had Katie touched him casually over the years? A million. A hand on the arm. An arm slung around his shoulder. Jumping on his back for a piggyback ride. Tackling him during a light game of football at one of the Dawsons' many parties in their huge backyard.

Never had an electric current zapped from the place of contact to his toes and then radiated everywhere in his body. *Everywhere.*

"Well, I got my best friend back and became a dad all on the same day," he said fast, trying to shake this new awareness of her as an actual woman and not just his bestie.

"And I got my best friend back and got to introduce the twins to their dad. So yeah, I'd say it was an amazing day."

He pulled into a spot in front of BabyCenter, the huge store with its multicolored giant sign of a baby in a diaper.

"While I was at the police station I found out that my bank accounts will be unfrozen. I don't have a ton of money, but I was always a saver, so it'll be nice to be less nervous about every penny I spend on the boys."

"I'd like to make up for lost time on all counts," he said as he came around the side of the SUV to open her door. "You had to be their sole source of support for three months. It's my turn."

She gave his hand a squeeze, then hopped out and they each went to a side to take out a baby. Katie had Declan, and Asher had Dylan.

"So this shopping trip is on me, Katie," he said, giving Dylan's cheek a nuzzle as he closed the door with his elbow. "Not just anything they need—anything you want for them. You went without for so long. Now, if the most indulgent baby product catches your eye, I want you to have it. Rex's wife, Maisey, told me a mom at the ranch day care insists on a baby wipes warmer for her infant's tush."

Katie laughed. "Well, I don't think that'll be on my list. I have one running in my head. I was always about saving time and money. And waiting for a baby wipe to warm up? Nah."

"I'm with you," he said.

They headed inside and put the twins in the infant baby seats of a special shopping cart designed for twins, Asher pushing while Katie let her eyes roam and her free hands explore the items.

"Ooh, look at this," she said, pointing at a baby rocker with a lullaby player and a mobile. "It's exactly the kind of thing I couldn't afford on my own, let alone have room for."

"We have plenty of room now," he said. He took two of the big boxes down from the shelf and stored them on the underside of the cart.

Katie smiled and he was happy to see her eyes light up when they headed to the clothing section. So many cute little outfits and pj's. She took two of the fleece winter suits with "Cowboy in Training" written on a patch on the chest. Asher grabbed two little brown Stetsons. By the time they left that section, the twins had a brand-new wardrobe. Then some new bottles and delicious smelling baby wash and soft fluffy towels with hoods in the shape of a bear's head. Asher went a little overboard in the toy section, but as he put it, "I've been a father for two days. I'll calm down about wanting to give them everything eventually. Or not."

As they were heading to the cash register, Declan started to fuss. Katie was about to pick him up, but Asher beat her to it, hoisting his son high in the air, the baby's legs giving little kicks, one of the twins' latest milestones. He cradled Declan against his chest, earning an "aww" from two women passing by with a zapper gun the store used for baby registries.

"Such a beautiful family," the older woman

said, smiling at Declan snuggled up against Asher. "How old are your twins?"

"Three months," Asher said. The woman smiled warmly and moved on. "That's the second time today that someone referred to us as a family," he said to Katie.

"Well, we are. You've always been my family, Ash."

He looked at her. "And you mine."

"And the twins are our family. You and me both."

After this, they'd head over to the county courthouse to apply for the twins' birth certificates. His name as father. Declan and Dylan Dawson. They *were* a family.

Asher nodded slowly as if thinking about something. Like maybe the idea of proposing.

Her heart soared a bit, and if he asked her to marry him—for the twins' sake and so he could keep the ranch—right at the checkout in Baby-Center, that would be just fine with her. More than fine. She'd jump for joy.

But by the time the clerk had rung up all their purchases, there was no proposal. Not on the way back to Asher's SUV or at the courthouse—and they'd been there awhile, Katie showing forms from the clinic in Thornberry and speaking to a supervisor about the delay in filing for birth certificates—or during the ride back to the ranch.

We are a family. And you need to keep this ranch. Ask me to marry you, darn it!

She willed it to him as they got out of the SUV and took Declan from his car seat, Asher bringing all the heavy stuff inside before taking out Dylan.

But once they got inside, each of them carrying a baby, Asher said, "So I've been thinking about something."

Katie almost gasped.

This had to be it.

Unless he was about to say he'd been thinking about dinner or if she'd like to take the evening barn chores and he'd do bedtime for the twins.

Could they be about to rewind to a year ago but have it go differently? The fresh start she'd been dreaming of since she'd been alone in that little cabin with her infants, scared and worried but hopeful about the future and the surprises it could hold?

"Oh?" she asked, holding her breath.

Chapter Six

Katie stood still, barely breathing. Waiting.

Propose, propose, propose.

Asher looked at the baby snuggled against him, then at Dylan in Katie's arms before holding her gaze. "I know that given what I said last year, how upset I made you, I have no right to ask this of you. But now it's not just about saving the ranch. It's about these two," he added, wagging a finger between the babies.

Oh my. Her heart lifted with such hope that her knees felt a little wobbly.

Katie kept her expression neutral. She didn't want to appear too happy and give him the idea that this was her Christmas wish. Sure, the marriage would come first, *then* the slow courtship until the depth of their feelings for each other were impossible for him to deny. Okay fine, that was her real Christmas wish.

But sometimes, things happened backward or in the supposed wrong order.

"Why don't we both sit down," he suggested and she could see he was giving himself a minute.

She went into the living room and sat on the sofa, Dylan on her lap. He sat beside her, angled toward her, Dylan smiling and giggling at his brother.

"Suddenly, keeping this ranch in the family means something even greater now that we have the twins, Katie. This is their family history, their legacy, something special to be passed down to them. Getting married so we can keep the ranch and for the sake of our children makes a lot of sense."

"My answer was yes when it was just about the ranch and you," she said. "So of course it's yes now that we have the babies to think about."

Relief lit up his eyes. "You hear that, Declan? You hear that, Dylan? Your mama said yes."

She smiled. This was a good start. They were beginning from a place of emotion—not a business arrangement.

"Last year, when I called off the engagement, I was worried about our friendship getting destroyed," he said. "I saw what one night of sex did to us, Katie. We didn't talk for a month. And even when we repaired our friendship, things were awkward and strained. Nothing can come between us now. Our partnership is *everything*. So we'll just be the best friends we've always been. Once the year is up and the ranch is officially ours, we can decide how to proceed."

Katie tried to keep her frown off her face. What the hell? Once the year was up, they would decide how to proceed? How deep could his feelings run if he was already thinking of ending their marriage the minute they legally could without jeopardizing the ranch?

Where was Gigi and her optimistic explanations for everything Asher-related right now?

She knew what Gigi would say, though. That she and Asher just had to take this one step at a time. Starting with a first step down the aisle. Then she'd have a year inside a beautiful marriage and sweet family to show Asher what was really between them. The way he'd suddenly leaned toward her in the bar the night they'd ended up in bed hadn't just been a lusty look at her and an impulse to kiss her; she'd seen everything in his eyes in that moment. If she were honest, she'd say she'd seen love. *Romantic* love. Desire. Tenderness. Respect. Years of incredible chemistry that had finally ignited into that hot kiss that had led them out of the bar and to the apartment she'd rented just a few blocks away.

Yes, they'd opened another bottle of wine like idiots and unfortunately Katie couldn't even remember all the great parts of the night. But she remembered the way he'd kissed her in her kitchen after they'd clinked glasses. *To getting through life with a friend as great as you*, was his toast. Katie should have recognized the sign that he was still operating on a friendship level and that the alcohol was responsible for everything else, not any deep buried romantic feelings.

None of this mattered now, she reminded herself. They had twin three-month-old sons. They were what mattered. The babies and keeping the ranch.

"We'll make this work," she assured him.

"I get my best friend, my sons and the ranch," he said. "I can't believe it. How did I get so damned lucky, after all?"

Yes, she thought, trying not to let her hopeful heart run away. This was a very good start.

"And I get to give this back to you," he said, pulling a black velvet box from his pocket.

She withheld the gasp. When he'd brought out that box the first time around, she'd almost burst into tears—of joy, of shock, of the reality that the marriage wasn't exactly the real thing. The first time around, the ring meant something huge—

a commitment to each other—and she had high hopes that she could show him what they had, that she could blast through whatever had been keeping her in the friend zone all these years. She'd been convinced that his parents' many marriages and his own heartaches had put the idea in his head that to keep their friendship forever, to never ruin it, there could never be anything romantic between them. If she could get him to see that a combination of the two could make for the most beautiful, strongest, most lasting relationship...

But then he'd ended the engagement. "Taking that ring off my finger and giving it back to you was among the hardest things I've ever done," she said. "It made me feel like I couldn't help you. That you weren't letting me help you. So what kind of best friend did that make me?"

He tilted his head, his expression turning somber. "I didn't even think of that. That you'd see it that way. I'm so sorry for the past, Katie." He took the beautiful diamond ring in its gold setting from the box and slid it on her finger. "To righting wrongs. To a second chance. To friendship."

She was careful not to grimace, though it was bursting from her cheeks. "To our family, Asher. Because that's what we are now."

And that was the truth. No matter what happened between them, they would always be a family.

"To family," he said, glancing from one twin to the other, then back at her.

And to us, she silently added. *And Christmas wishes coming true.*

One of her wishes had already come true. She'd been able to come home, with Declan and Dylan, and reunite with Asher. That made her feel blessed enough. But her hope for her and Asher to become a real couple, to have a real marriage, was burning bright.

That they were engaged again, with a lot more at stake this time around, had Asher kind of unsettled, so he'd excused himself to go take down the for-sale signs from the road and by the drive. Pulling up the signs felt damned good. He called the Realtor and let her know the ranch was off the market. That felt even better. Then he'd called his grandmother's lawyer and let him know he would be married by Christmas and would not be selling the ranch, after all. The stipulations of the will would be met. Even the attorney had cheered and said he was thrilled to hear the news, that his grandmother would have been overjoyed.

As Asher turned toward the barn to get the afternoon chores done, he watched the goats in the pasture, his chest and shoulders unknotting.

I'm not going to disappoint you, after all, Gram, he thought, turning his face skyward.

In the barn, he got Plum Pudding up on the milking stand that his grandfather had built fifty years ago when he and Cassie had started the goat ranch. The hay bag was hung up with some grain nestled inside as a special treat for the goats to eat while he worked. He liked milking the goats, always had, and the past year, he'd enjoyed filling the mason jars with his grandmother's label and then loading them up to deliver to the various grocery stores and specialty shops that sold Dawson's Sweet Dairy Ranch milk products. All the vendors and customers always commented on how missed Cassie was. She sure was.

When he was almost finished milking Plum Pudding he opened up the hay bag so that she could eat, then filtered and poured the milk into jars and stored them in the barn refrigerator. He repeated this with other does. As he let the last one join the others in the pasture, he swept out the pen and set out fresh hay.

He heard a car coming up the long drive, finished up in the barn and headed outside. The bright red pickup meant it was his father. John Dawson was more a silver or gray truck type, but his wife, Mandy, liked color. The couple had met in a park where Mandy had a booth to sell her healing stones, crystals and essential oils; they'd eloped to Vegas within a month and settled in the large cabin just under an hour away that had been her family home and had held her father's guiding business. Now it was a small healing spa.

Asher shielded his eyes from the setting sun but was pretty sure Mandy wasn't in the passenger seat. The couple, married for just under a year, were attached at the hip, so it was unusual for his dad to go anywhere without his wife. This past year, whenever he thought of his father, which honestly wasn't all that often, he'd been strangely comforted by the fact that even though Asher had only met Mandy once, *she'd* met Katie: at his grandmother's funeral.

He'd felt a connection to his new stepmother for that simple reason. The Dawsons hadn't stuck around too long after the funeral, but Mandy had been kind and warm and he'd heard her telling Katie that she had old soul eyes and an aura of peace about her. Asher didn't go much for that stuff, but Katie liked what Mandy had said and often commented on Katie's peaceful aura with a smile. He'd invited the couple to the ranch a few times the past year but his father always had an excuse. John Dawson had hated growing up on the goat ranch and he wasn't the least bit upset about not having inherited the place or any stake in it. Asher hadn't even bothered telling him about the stipulation of the will, since his father would tell him to just let the estate sell it and be done with it. He was glad he'd pulled up the signs before his dad had arrived; that was lucky timing.

He walked up to the truck. "Dad? Surprised to see you here." He always felt a little jolt when he saw his dad; the two of them looked a lot alike. His father had the same thick dark hair, albeit salt and pepper threading through, the same intense blue eyes and the strong jawline. They were both six two, and his father was in very good physical shape.

"Mandy left me," his father said, his expression bleak. "She says I act like the honeymoon is over and that that's a deal breaker for her. But the honeymoon literally ended a year ago. I'm missing something but I don't know what."

Asher sighed inwardly. He might have thought something unkind about his father's failures in relationships—this was marriage number four—but he could plainly see John Dawson was a wreck right now. Why he'd sought out his son, who'd never married and had a long list of failed relationships himself, was a mystery. He and his father had never been particularly close either.

"She says *I* can 'worry about the spa for once,'" his dad said. "But that's her domain. I don't know anything about healing crystals or Reiki! I handle the business end."

"And you drove up here instead of holding down the fort because…" Asher prompted.

His father was flustered and Asher suddenly felt bad for judging him. "I was just so beside myself I didn't know what to do. I just started driving and found myself needing to come here, be on familiar soil. And I thought maybe you'd have some advice for me."

"Me?" Asher said.

"What do I do, Ash?" his father repeated.

"Hi, Mr. Dawson," came Katie's voice, and they both turned around.

"Wait—*what*?" John Dawson said, staring at Katie. "Okay, I have to be seeing things. Or I'm in the middle of a bad dream and Katie's ghost is after me for messing things up with Mandy." He took a step back, his eyes wide then narrowing on Katie, then wide again.

"I'm really here, Mr. Dawson," Katie said. She briefly explained what happened. "I'm just glad I got to come home before Christmas."

His father gave her a hug. "Wow. Wow! That is some story. Well, welcome home, Katie. I remember when you were a tiny girl running around the ranch with Asher, and I was so sad when he told me the news you were gone. I'm real happy you're not."

Katie smiled. "Thanks, Mr. Dawson."

"And there's something else you should know, Dad," Asher said. "You're a grandfather. Of twin three-month-old boys."

John Dawson's mouth dropped open. "I'm a grandpa? You're a dad?"

"I am. Another surprise that Katie had for me. Come on in and meet them. And we can talk more about what's going on with you and Mandy." He glanced at Katie, who seemed to instantly understand from that last bit that there was trouble in paradise.

As Katie pulled open the storm door, John Dawson stopped in his tracks.

Katie turned around. "Everything okay?"

"Do I see an engagement ring on your finger?" John asked.

"I think you're the first to know, Dad," Asher said. "We just got engaged today."

"Isn't that wonderful!" John said. "Picking up right where you left off. I'm so happy for you both." But then his father frowned. "And here I am, full of marital problems and heaping them on you. I should probably get going. Today is about celebration. You don't need me bringing you guys down."

That was thoughtful of the man. John Dawson usually put himself first.

"You come right in," Katie said, wrapping her arm around his. "I'm sorry to hear you and Mandy are having problems. I only met her that one time, under sad circumstances at your mom's funeral, but I thought Mandy was such a warm, kind person."

John's face almost crumpled. "She is. I just don't know what I'm doing wrong. She says *everything*."

"Oh boy," Asher said.

"The twins will wake up from their nap in about twenty minutes or so," Katie said. "Why don't we sit down to coffee. Asher has some great cookies too."

"Sounds good," John said. "Haven't been here in a while," he added, looking around.

His father didn't know about the stipulation in his mother's will or that he and Katie were marrying for less than romantic reasons—again—and there seemed no reason to tell him. Especially in his dad's state of mind right now, it seemed better to keep that to themselves.

"I'll go get the coffee," Asher said.

Katie shot him a smile, then sat down beside his father on the sofa. For a moment, Asher just stared at the two of them, his chest full. He'd never expected to see Katie again, and to have his father make a rare appearance in town, in this house he had no interest in, the combination had Asher all...emotional. One of his dad's many mottos had always been to expect the unexpected, and that definitely applied here.

"So, Mr. Dawson," Katie said, "what's going on with you and Mandy if you don't mind me just asking?"

"Oh, I don't mind at all. I'm hoping for guidance. And please call me John. I'm not a 'Mr. Dawson' type. And besides, we're going to be family."

Asher hit Brew on the coffee maker and got out the mugs and tray with cream and sugar and a plate of the good bakery cookies he'd picked up the other day.

"She says I take her for granted," his dad lamented. "That this feeling has been building up in her for the last month and that I don't listen when she tries to tell me stuff. She's gone off to her sister's a half hour away and left me to handle the spa. I take care of the finances. But I can't run the actual spa."

"So you left the spa on its own?" Asher called out as he poured three cups of coffee.

"Well, we have a good assistant manager. She's in charge while I'm gone. Gosh, I hope she doesn't tell Mandy I'm not there."

Asher sighed again.

Katie stood up. "John, I'll be right back. I'm just going to help Asher in the kitchen."

Asher was about to call out that he had it under control when Katie appeared in the kitchen with an expression on her face that he knew well. It meant she had an idea, one she was mulling over. He could tell by the half worried, half excited look in her eyes.

She took his hand and led him farther into the kitchen. "Ash," she whispered. "I just thought of a way we could help your dad and take care of some personal business at the same time."

He tilted his head, no clue what she could be referring to.

"We need to get married, right?" she continued, voice low. "Of course it'll be just a simple ceremony since it's not, I mean since we're not— What I'm trying to say is, despite everything, I don't want to get married at the town hall in an impersonal ceremony by the mayor, who isn't a very nice person, by the way."

That was true; the new mayor was a real blowhard. But Asher *did* like the idea of getting married at the town hall. For exactly the reason she mentioned: it would be impersonal. And wasn't *impersonal* the way to go in this kind of situation? When they were marrying for the sake of their babies and to keep the ranch?

Except, there was nothing impersonal about marriage. No matter the reason for it.

"Last year, Mandy told me a little about the spa and it sounds lovely," Katie said. "We could get married *there*—with your dad and Mandy as our witnesses. In fact, if I'm remembering right, Mandy is an ordained minister and could do the ceremony. That would certainly bring her back home. And maybe a wedding will get the two of them really talking. It'll remind both of them what they have and what they stand to lose."

Asher nodded slowly as he thought it over. Getting his family involved made him a little uneasy but then again, he and his father had never been very close and he barely knew Mandy. That fit right in with *impersonal*. But more importantly, Katie was right. It was a good plan. If he could help out his dad, he would.

"I'm in," he said. Talk about impersonal. But that was all that would come out of his mouth. The past couple of days had been a whirlwind. A shocking whirlwind. He wasn't so sure adding his dad and his marital issues to the mix would help *himself*, but Christmas was about giving, so…

Katie's smile went straight to his heart. "Good. Then we have a plan. A secret plan. I like that."

"Should we invite your mother and her husband?" Katie asked. "Or will that be very complicated?"

"My mother and David have been traveling the South in an RV and are leaving tomorrow, I think, for a monthlong European cruise until after New Year's, so no worries about her feelings. I haven't even called to tell her she's a grandmother because it's not like she'd rush home to see the twins. I'll let her know when she's back." He and his mother had a nice enough relationship, but like with his father, they'd never been particularly close.

"Okay, then," Katie said, picking up the plate of cookies. "Let's go talk to your dad."

Asher took the tray with the coffee and they headed back into the living room. He set the tray on the coffee table, then sat on the love seat across from the sofa.

"John, I was thinking," Katie said as she sat back down beside him. "When I met Mandy last November, she described the spa and how pretty it is, and Asher and I were just talking about how nice it would be to have our small wedding there. Do you think Mandy would agree to be our officiant? It wouldn't be a big affair—the guest list would be you and the twins. That's it."

John's eyes lit up. "When would the wedding be? Soon?"

Katie smiled. "This weekend?" she said in the form of a question, looking at Asher. "Saturday afternoon?"

His collar felt like it had tightened. Had she said *this* Saturday? Today was Tuesday. Then again, they had to marry before Christmas. So they might as well make it legal this weekend. "Saturday afternoon sounds good to me. Dad?"

"Let me call Mandy," John said excitedly, popping up and hurrying out of the room.

Asher took a long drink of his coffee. "How do

you think the conversation is going?" he asked, nodding toward the doorway his father had disappeared through.

"I have a good feeling about this," she said, taking a bite of a chocolate chip cookie. "It's a little sneaky on our part but it helps us and it helps them."

"Saturday, huh?" he said. "That's coming right up."

"Sure is."

"I suppose we should talk about the ceremony, then. I'll wear a suit."

"And I'll wear a wedding-ish dress. Not a full-blown gown, of course, but something bridal."

He nodded. "Well, anything you want or need for the ceremony is fine by me," he said. "Thank you," he added. "If I didn't say that earlier. For marrying me."

"Well, now it's for both of us, right? So thank *you*, Ash."

He leaned back and sipped his coffee. *Both of us.* Yes. He just had to remember that they were marrying for the right reasons if that in itself seemed backward. The right reason to marry was love, wasn't it? And his father, on marriage number four, which was in serious trouble after barely a year, was proof that love—being *in love*—wasn't the only reason to make someone your partner in life.

Katie stretched up her arms, letting out a yawn, her red sweater inching up to reveal a creamy swath of her stomach. "I'm trying to nap less these days now that the twins are sleeping for a good six-hour stretch, but I still get so tired during the day."

"Anytime you need a nap, I've got the twins. Just say the word."

"I appreciate that, Asher."

He shook his head. "No appreciation necessary. Knowing you have someone to count on 24/7, the other parent, is new to you after three months on your own. I'm there for them with everything I've got and that goes for you too."

Her eyes got misty. "How'd you know what I want for Christmas?"

He smiled and gave her hand a squeeze.

John Dawson came dashing back into the living room, a smile on his face. "Mandy will be back Friday afternoon! She's thrilled about you two wanting her to officiate the ceremony. She'd love for you both to come Friday night and make a weekend of it. She said to give her a call when you've got a moment today to go over what you envision." He turned to Asher. "I think you have Mandy's number."

"I do," Asher said.

I do. I do. I do. He swallowed. Everything

would be okay. He just had to focus on what was important. Not his unease.

Katie smiled. "Great. Then it's all set. And how nice that Mandy will be back, especially for such a joyous occasion as a wedding. That just might help things between you two," she added. "Weddings have a way of making people think about how they really feel."

"I sure hope so," John said. "Well, then, I'd better get back to the spa and take care of business. I want to make sure Mandy knows I'm there and keeping the place running."

"Good idea, Dad," Asher said, standing up.

"Oh, wait, I didn't get to meet the twins," John said, frowning.

"You can meet them Friday. Just a few more days. It'll be nice for you and Mandy to meet them together."

John's face lit up. "That's true. Something for us to share together."

Asher nodded and walked his dad to the door, Katie following.

"See you Friday," Katie said, giving John a hug. "I think things are going to be just fine. Just keep an open ear and open mind. Women like to be listened to. And heard."

"I've never been great at that," John said. "Asher can vouch for that."

Asher was about to say, *Yes, I can*, but he didn't.

Instead, he clapped his dad on the shoulder. "See you Friday. Drive safely."

His father's face was full of purpose and renewed energy as he practically flew out the door to his pickup. With a hand on the door, he glanced over at the pasture, where the goats were now congregating, Plum Pudding on her favorite log.

The man had grown up here but had left the ranch as soon as he could, renting a condo in town while he worked to put himself through college. Asher couldn't be more different than his dad. A ranch, and goats in particular, soothed Asher, felt like home. His dad preferred a business office—he was an accountant by trade—and had always complained that goats were smelly and would chew the hair off your head if you weren't looking.

He remembered something Katie had said more than once: *You've always been very different people. Don't be so hard on him for that. He doesn't have to be like you for you to love him.*

"Well, I'd better call Gigi, who knows everything about pulling a wedding together," Katie said.

He nodded and watched her head up the stairs, wishing she was back here with him. He flashed back to prom night, Katie in that pretty pink satin dress with the flounce around her knees. He'd watched her spin around on the dance floor before

her date had turned into a total jerk, and Asher
had been entranced for a moment.

She'd always meant a little too much to him
and that was just plain scary. Even when she was
strictly his best friend. Not also his wife-to-be.
Not also the mother of his children.

Suddenly, dealing with his father's love life issues seemed like a piece of cake.

Chapter Seven

Katie woke up in the morning feeling so refreshed. As if she'd slept through the entire night. She glanced at her phone on the bedside table. Almost seven o'clock. She bolted up. That meant Asher had taken care of the twins during the night if they'd woken, and they likely had. And he was probably with them right now. Letting her sleep in.

Last night, he'd made dinner, chicken burritos that were delicious, and they'd eaten in the kitchen, talking about his dad and Mandy and then about his cousins, then about the goats and going full speed ahead on the milk and cheese production, which she was excited about taking on, and then of course, the twins. They'd covered just about every topic except the marriage, and Katie did have questions. Lots of questions.

But somehow they seemed unanswerable out of context. They would just have to see how things felt, how things were, she figured. They'd have separate bedrooms, of course, since it wasn't a real marriage. She didn't even need to double-check on that.

But she could hope that their shared life would bring them closer in ways Asher never expected... and that they'd be sharing a bedroom and a sex life by Valentine's Day. She'd drifted off to sleep last night imagining just that. And remembering their one night together last November.

This morning, she and Gigi were going shopping for their wedding dresses. They'd texted back and forth for almost an hour last night about all that had happened yesterday, Katie filling in her friend on the engagement and the spa location for the ceremony—and how worried she was that her soon-to-be husband would never see her as anything other than his bestie. Gigi, a total romantic who'd gotten to know Asher pretty well over the years, had long thought the guy just didn't see what was right under his nose but absolutely would now that so much had changed.

So much *had* changed. Their one night together and all it had wrought. That he thought he'd lost her—for an entire year. That she was back in his life and the mother of his two baby sons. That they needed each other. Buoyed that Gigi could really be right, Katie headed downstairs.

Asher was in the kitchen, coffee made, the twins in their new bouncy seats. Asher keeping up a running commentary as he stood at the stove, making an omelet.

"Ah, there she is," he said, smiling at her. "Just in time for a western omelet and sourdough toast."

"I didn't even know I was craving that until you mentioned them. Yum."

"Coming right up," he said.

"I can run out to the barn and see what needs doing," she said. "I'm not used to being a lady of leisure. Waking up at seven. Having the twins cared for. Breakfast made for me. I like it, though." Boy, did she.

"Well, get used to it. Like I said, it's my turn, Katie. And I mean it. I already took care of the goats and the barn. The twins helped, didn't you, guys?" he asked, giving each of their noses a little tap. Both giggled and looked up at him. "I took them in the double stroller and they were mesmerized by the goats."

She smiled. And when he slid the plate of an omelet and toast in front of her, along with butter and her favorite apricot jam and her coffee just the way she liked it, she thought she might be dreaming.

But then she remembered that their marriage would make them just roommates sharing a home and babies, and she came back down to earth very quickly.

"Gigi's picking you up at nine?" he asked.

She nodded. "We'll be having two very different weddings, but it's still nice to shop together. I missed her so much this past year." She took a bite of her omelet—heavenly—and looked at him. "You really don't mind that I'll be gone for hours?"

"Not at all. Happy to have the twins to myself."

"They're so lucky that you're their dad, Asher. How you've instantly taken to being a father and to them, it's just beautiful."

"Well, I know that my own dad wasn't around much, even when he was still married to my mother. And then I hardly saw him, despite him not having more kids. I plan to be there for my children. I want them to know they're loved. I want them to grow up with that as natural to them as breathing."

"That's what I want for them too," she said, feeling her eyes getting all misty. "You know, maybe our weekend trip to the spa won't just bring your dad and Mandy back together. Maybe it'll give you and your father some needed time together. You *can* get closer now, you know."

"I doubt that'll happen, Katie. There's just not a lot there between us. I love him. I care about him. But we really don't have a relationship. And that's fine. I'm used to it."

But it didn't have to be that way. And a closer relationship with his dad might undo some long-held beliefs about love and family that he didn't even know kept him from being as happy as he could be.

After breakfast, Katie did the dishes, which she had to insist on, and then she played with the twins in the living room, a little tummy time, a few rounds of peekaboo, all the while talking their ear off about how their parents would be getting married this weekend and they would be there. She was so aware of Asher lying on the floor beside them, his head propped by an elbow, listening to her running commentary, that she was careful about what she said. The last time she wasn't careful about what had come out of her mouth in the name of honesty, he'd canceled the engagement. She didn't think that would happen again, even if he could read her mind and find out just how in love with him she was, had always been.

Even if now there was wariness mixed with her optimism. They could have something truly amazing together. Or they could be friends. Housemates. At this moment in time, he was stuck on friends. That just meant she had her work cut out for her if she wanted to make her Christmas dreams come true.

He was so close to her on the floor that he could just reach over and kiss her, look deeply into her eyes, and then gaze lovingly at their baby boys...

By the time she heard Gigi's car pull up, she was in a full-blown fantasy of wearing a Cinderella gown for the wedding, walking down the aisle to her waiting groom, who was madly in love with her.

But as Asher said hello to Gigi and held up each twin for Katie to kiss goodbye before carrying them both back into the living room where he started telling them a story about a baby goat named Dipsy, she knew that it was the boys who had his heart. Not her. And she was mentally back to the side racks for her dress, something tea length and not white or very bridal.

Since the Bear Ridge Police Department was holding the "Welcome Home, Katie Crosby" tribute tomorrow morning, Katie figured she'd keep a low profile until then, when it was truly public that she was back. And alive. So she and Gigi, who had today off, decided to drive the forty-five minutes to Brewster, which had two bridal boutiques. Katie wasn't sure she'd find the right dress in a bridal shop, but Gigi had assured her that the bridal party racks held all sorts of dresses.

"I have no idea *what* I'm looking for," she told her friend as they pulled open the door to the first bridal boutique, which was all pale pink and white, and beautiful gowns everywhere. "I think I'll know it when I see it."

She was marrying the love of her life. The man of her dreams.

Her best friend.

The dress had to be special. No matter what.

Gigi headed toward the gowns while Katie went left to the bridal party racks. She slid hanger after hanger, nothing catching her eye. Rack after rack. Gigi, on the other hand, had let out a few gasps, a saleswoman quickly coming over to take the gowns into a fitting room while she kept looking through the beautiful creations.

"No luck yet?" Gigi asked, two more gowns hanging over her arm.

"Not yet. Lots of beauties, though. Just not the one."

"I've found eight 'the ones.' And there's another shop. So if you don't see it here, we'll find it somewhere else."

The saleswoman called Gigi over to try on her haul, and Katie kept looking through the racks.

"Katie," Gigi called from inside the dressing room, her voice sounding funny.

Katie hurried over. "Everything okay?" she asked through the door.

Silence.

"Gigi?" Katie said, wondering what was wrong.

The door opened and Katie stepped back. Gigi had tears in her eyes as she headed toward the three-way mirror across the hall. It wasn't until Katie glanced down at the gown, at her friend in the gown, that she realized why Gigi had had such a reaction.

"Oh, Gigi," Katie breathed, hand going to her mouth.

She looked so beautiful, like the dress had been made for her skin tone and figure and personality. The satin beaded white ball gown was strapless and so utterly perfect that Katie couldn't speak.

The more she stared at her dear friend in that beautiful dress, the more she understood that she wouldn't be having a moment like this. A moment she'd thought about a lot over the years. Back when she was in middle school and her crush on Asher in full bloom, she'd pictured the two of them at their wedding in the park where they often hung out, Katie in a princess ball gown with a long veil, tulle galore. In high school, the dress changed to something more Academy Awards red

and she stepped into a pair of satin ecru pumps in the dressing room and then slipped the floaty dress over her head. It fit perfectly, draping over the roundness of her tummy.

"Gigi," she barely managed to whisper.

"Omigod, you're me now," Gigi called. "Can I see?"

Katie stepped out and now it was Gigi's turn to gasp.

"One and done," Gigi said. "It's just that kind of day. You look absolutely beautiful."

She would add the gold bracelet her father had left her, all he had really, which had belonged to his mother, the grandmother she'd never known.

"Nothing friend zone about you in that dress," Gigi said, nodding.

Nope, Katie thought, looking at her reflection, her heart suddenly soaring with the possibilities. There were three weeks till Christmas. She and Asher would be married. A family. Everything that was already so changed in their relationship would be changed all the more—deeper, richer, both of them in brand-new territory.

A lot could happen in three weeks.

Just three days ago, the sight of Christmas lights had filled Asher with dread. Today, he'd strung white lights around the front door, hung the huge wreath with its red bow atop the barn as his grandmother had done as long as he could remember, and was now elbow deep in the box of Christmas supplies in the attic. The twins were in their baby carriers, watching him intently, all big gummy smiles as he pulled out ornaments that had meant something to him as a kid.

"Now you guys will have these," he said. "On your own tree. Not that I want to think of you all grown up."

It was the family history, the legacy, something to carry on with for his sons that had gripped Asher.

He heard the front door open and Katie call out, "Asher, I'm back," and he felt himself light up like a Christmas tree. He'd missed her. Katie had been gone for hours, and after the first two had passed, he realized how much he wanted to see her.

"In the attic," he called down. "With my Christmas elves."

Her face appeared at the top of the stairs. "I missed you two so much!" She came in and picked up each baby, giving them a snuggle and a kiss on the head before slipping them back in their carriers. "We had a very successful day."

"Glad to hear it," he said.

"And I see you've been busy. The place looks great. So festive."

"I went from not being able to look at garland

wrapped around a light post in town to having my best friend back. To keeping the ranch. To having these guys in my life. That is something to celebrate."

Declan started to fuss, then Dylan began rubbing his eyes.

"I should have put them down for their naps twenty minutes ago," he said, "but I got caught up in looking through all this Christmas stuff my grandmother packed away. Lots of good memories in here.

"Remember this?" he asked, pulling out an evergreen-shaped ornament with a little photo of him and Katie in the star atop it. Katie had made it at a craft booth for kids when they were in elementary school.

"And this," she said, her hand going to her heart as she pulled out another ornament, a brown-and-white Australian shepherd with a red-and-green collar.

He stared at the ornament. They'd once found a stray Australian shepherd and both had fallen in love with it, but his grandmother had been allergic to dogs and Katie couldn't have a dog at the foster home. They always used to say that when they were out on their own, they'd each adopt an Australian shepherd, their favorite breed of dog, and walk them together in the park, Asher always casually adding, *Even if when we're married to other people. Friends forever.*

"Neither of us ever did adopt a dog," she said.

His work at his cousins' ranch and helping out his grandmother here had made that too difficult. And Katie had always worked full-time. "Maybe we could finally adopt one."

She tilted her head. "Really?"

"Yeah. It'll be like a Christmas present for the family we're forming."

She shot into his arms, wrapping hers around him. "Oh, Asher. I would love that."

He looked down at her, unable to even think about removing his arms from her body. She felt so good. So good.

He looked into her eyes, the pale brown so familiar, as were the delicate bit of freckles across her nose and the full pink-red lips that were suddenly so mesmerizing. He couldn't stop staring at her or step away or remove himself from the embrace.

And she wasn't moving either.

But then Declan started crying. And Dylan joined him.

He snapped to reality—and stepped back. Katie did too, looking uncomfortable.

She turned to the twins and picked up Declan's carrier. "Time for two little someones' naps."

He took Dylan's carrier and followed her down the stairs and into the nursery.

She changed each twin and then laid them down in their bassinets. He was grateful she was taking charge because he couldn't even think straight. What had just happened up there? Had he been attracted to Katie? Seriously attracted? To the point that he couldn't drag his eyes off her face? He'd loved the feel of her in his arms—and he'd hugged her a zillion times over the years.

This was no ordinary hug. This was charged with something that felt a lot like desire. On both their parts.

He walked over to the bassinets and looked down at his sons. *Nothing can come between your mom and me,* he silently said to them. *Nothing can tear us apart. I can't risk that. We've got to be about family. Partnership. Not...lust.* Sex destroyed friendships. It had almost destroyed them once.

And romance? It just never worked out. With his mother on husband three and his dad on wife four—a marriage that was on the rocks—Asher wasn't about to let this unexpected flare of attraction ruin the best thing he had in this world. He'd just gotten Katie back. No way would he do anything to lose her again. To arguments. To strange expectations. Sex and romance were great—but they led to breaking up. Always had and Asher was thirty years old.

He nodded to himself, his head back on straight. Katie was about to become his wife. But there could be nothing more than friendship between them.

Chapter Eight

Yesterday, Katie had felt the change come over Asher, that beautiful, unexpected moment between them in the attic shifting to awkward in record time. He hadn't really recovered all last night. Tight smiles. Making himself scarce. Spending a lot of time on the phone with his cousins, telling them about the wedding this weekend. Katie's heart sinking with the stilted tone of his voice. *A big party to celebrate when we get back sounds great,* she'd heard him say. *We'll plan something in a couple weeks. I think Katie would love a big festive party.*

Yesterday, before the attic moment, that he knew what she loved and could speak for her would have made her happy. Afterward, a weight pressed down. Why had she flung herself into his arms like that? She'd just been so moved about the idea of them adopting a dog that she'd acted without thinking.

But so had he. And that was straight-up desire she'd seen burning in his blue eyes. He'd never looked at her like that before. Except that one night last November when they'd both had way too much to drink and she'd been forced to chalk up his sudden interest in her to very strong margaritas. This was different. He'd wanted her in the attic. She had no doubt. And by the time she got the twins settled, he was *unsettled*, the moment long gone and something changed again between them.

One step forward, two back, but that's the way it goes until you get there, she thought, trying to give herself a pep talk.

She sat at the kitchen table and sipped her coffee. It was early, not quite 5:30 a.m., and she'd already cleaned the goat pasture, fed them, gave them fresh hay and grain, and had two cups of coffee. Upstairs was silent. The twins had woken up once during the night, but as she'd thrown off the covers, she'd heard Asher's door opening and his lighthearted voice in the nursery. *Which one of you is making this unholy racket at 2:10?*

She'd wanted to join them, but she'd stayed put, pulling the comforter back over herself.

Now she heard fussing from upstairs and was about to head up but she also heard Asher talking, doors opening and closing, his running commentary as he changed them and started coming down the hall. "Wait till you guys get to try pancakes for the first time," he was saying. "With maple syrup and a side of blueberries. Chocolate chip pancakes are my favorite."

I know, she thought wistfully, remembering how many times he'd ordered exactly that at the Bear Ridge Diner over the years when they'd go for breakfast.

When he entered the kitchen, a baby in each arm, she was so emotional she couldn't even stand up to say good morning to him and the twins. He gave her a pleasant enough smile, but she could easily see the strain on his face as he focused on the babies, getting them in their high chairs before going over to the coffee maker.

"Ready for the big morning?" he asked sitting down beside her and sipping his coffee.

At 10:00 a.m., the Bear Ridge Police Department would be hosting a short welcome home tribute ceremony to Katie for her bravery in the face of adversity. The story was now out on the town's social media feeds, and Katie had done a few short interviews over email and the telephone yesterday. *You very likely saved several lives*, a reporter from the *Bear Ridge Gazette* had said. *The ex-con was dangerous and clearly meant her threats.*

Katie was just glad it was all behind her. She'd lost a year of the life she'd planned, she'd lost her career, for now, at least, but she'd found out just how strong she was during all those months in hiding. And she had her boys.

Before she could even answer, Asher got up and rooted around in the refrigerator and the cabinets. He pulled out a box of Apple Cinnamon Cheerios and the half gallon of milk, then ate standing up as he leaned against the counter.

He wants to be as far from me as possible, she thought.

So completely derailed by a hot hug. Hmm. Perhaps this wasn't something that should be getting her down. The man wasn't comfortable with the two of them as anything other than friends; he'd made that crystal clear. But things were happening between them whether he liked it or not.

And that was a good thing—the way she saw it.

It was progress, which everyone knew you couldn't stop.

She smiled to herself, feeling a lot better. She'd just have to see what happened. And so would he.

A half hour later, they were all bundled up in

their winter gear and headed out for the drive to the town hall. As they parked, Katie could think about only one thing—how glad she was they weren't having their wedding here. The building was nice enough, a two story with a limestone facade. But inside were industrial carpet, beige walls, long hallways and very practical goings-on—car registrations and property tax payments and car stickers for the town recycling center. The parking lot was pretty full, which was nice to see; she clearly had a lot of support and that buoyed her spirits.

The tribute was being held in the "ballroom" and when Katie and Asher walked in, Asher pushing the twins in their stroller, she was amazed to see hundreds of people sitting in the audience. The first rows were taken up by the Bear Ridge PD. She saw Asher's cousin Rex and Gigi in the front row. The chief and Ford were on the far side of the small stage where a microphone was set up. Katie and Asher walked over and the chief filled them in on his planned remarks and told Katie she could say a few words afterward. It would be short and simple, which was perfect, and then Katie could resume life again in Bear Ridge. Instead of a police officer, she'd be a wife and mother and a goat rancher. That all sounded pretty great.

Chief Harringer walked up onto the stage and

began the tribute, explaining what had led Katie into hiding. Then she and Asher and the twins were called up, and the chief shook their hands. Katie went to the podium and thanked everyone for coming and said how grateful she was to be home. She got a standing ovation, which she didn't expect, and several people came up to her to comment on what she'd gone through and how wonderful it was that she was home in time for Christmas, and how cute the babies were.

And then a woman who Katie hadn't seen in at least three years came slowly up to her, her expression unsure, her movements tentative.

Celia Crosby. Katie's mother.

But there was something different about Celia now. She looked...healthier. Stronger. Her complexion, usually so pale and almost gray, was now robust. Her teeth had been fixed; the two big chips Katie remembered were gone, and a missing canine restored. Her clothes no longer hung on her and instead of the ratty, short dress she'd last seen her mother wear, Celia wore a red-and-green-plaid sweater that looked quite festive, well-fitting jeans and brown leather boots. Her straight brown hair fell between her chin and shoulders, clean and brushed, a fringe of bangs making her look younger than her fifty-one years.

Katie stared at her, unable to believe she was looking at the same woman who, the last time

Katie had seen her, had begged for her money. Fifty, a hundred, whatever she could spare. She'd screamed obscenities when Katie said she'd pay anything for drug rehab but she would not enable her by giving her cash to spend on drugs. Her mother had been in and out of jail Katie's entire childhood and adulthood. Petty burglary and cons to support her drug habit.

"It's so good to see you. Alive and well," Celia said, her eyes getting misty. "I never thought I'd see you again."

Katie wasn't so sure either, even though she'd planned to resume keeping tabs on Celia as she'd done since she was a teenager. Sometimes she couldn't find a trail of her mother for months, and a few years back, two years had gone by since her mother had aliases.

But now, as she looked at Celia Crosby's face, the brown eyes much like her own, she felt that old flicker of the yearning she used to have— that one day, she and her mother would have a relationship. Not that she'd trust Celia. Ever. Not this person who'd made her and her father's life miserable and uncertain for years. This person who'd let Katie go into foster care at four years old when her father had died. This person who wouldn't sign away her parental rights so that Katie could be adopted despite her refusal to get clean, despite social workers begging her to let Katie have a stable family life.

Still, this person was her mother. And that was powerful stuff.

"When I thought you'd died," Celia said, "I fell apart. I mean, really fell apart. I thought I knew what rock bottom was, but I didn't. Not till I read that my daughter had been killed in a car accident. I thought I'd never be able to make amends, not that I knew how to then." She reached out a hand. "You're really here, though."

Katie reflexively stepped back, years of Celia's lies and manipulations and scary tactics so fresh in her mind.

"I have so much to make up for," Celia continued. "If you'll let me. A few days after I'd heard on the news that you were gone, a social worker helped me. She'd found me shivering in the park under a bench in an old holey sleeping bag. I cried and cried and told her my daughter was dead and I'd never get the chance to make things right, never be the mother my child deserved."

Katie stared at Celia, barely able to process what she was hearing.

"Turned out, the woman ran a shelter in Brewster. She'd also lost a daughter, but to drugs. She told me I could turn things around. Do right by you even though you were in heaven. My life would have purpose in tribute to you. She got through, Katie. It was hard, those first days and weeks. But I went to the police station in Bear Ridge and talked to your colleagues and they also helped me."

Huh. Katie didn't know that. Celia was now looking to the left, where Asher was standing with the twins in the stroller as he chatted with his cousins.

"I'm a grandmother," Celia said, her voice clogged with emotion.

A surge of protectiveness rose up in Katie to the point that she moved to the left to block her mother's path to the twins. Celia Crosby hadn't just been neglectful; she'd been dangerous. Just because the woman said she'd changed and looked a thousand times better than she ever had didn't mean Katie could trust her. Not with her babies.

"This is a lot to process," Katie said. "I'm glad you got clean. Very glad. And that you changed your life. But I don't really know you."

Celia frowned. "And that is my fault. I understand your hesitation and wariness. You have every right. I just want you to know that I really have changed. And I want to get to know you, Katie. If I can have this second chance, maybe I could be the grandmother to your twins that they deserve."

Before Katie could respond, Asher came over with the twins, standing beside her. "Sorry to interrupt," he said, smiling at Celia, "but these guys are beginning to fuss and it's definitely time for their nap."

Katie glanced around; she hadn't even realized so many people had left. "Asher, you remember my mother, Celia Crosby." She could see Asher's mouth slightly fall but he caught it before it dropped too far.

"Mrs. Crosby," he said. "It's nice to see you again. It's been a long time."

"Yes," Celia said. "I'm hoping to change that." She reached into the pocket of her wool peacoat and handed Katie a slip of paper. "This has my cell phone and address on it. I've been renting an apartment in town, right above the bakery, where I work."

Katie managed a tight smile, still not able to think clearly. Celia smiled at Asher, then at the twins, then reached out a hand to Katie's arm before turning and walking away. Katie watched her head out the main door.

"I need to sit down for a second," she said, moving over across the aisle to the row of folding chairs. She dropped down in one.

Asher hurried over with the stroller and pulled out a bottle of water from the basket. "Have a drink."

She gratefully accepted it and took a long slug, her throat parched.

"I can't believe that was your mother," Asher said. "Wow."

"I know. I can't believe it either." She told Asher everything Celia had said.

"Lots of unexpected twists and turns this Christmas," he said. "A lot for you to think about."

She nodded, her gaze moving from his handsome face to the twins. A grandmother was a wonderful thing for children to have. But Katie was hardly willing to let Celia Crosby into their lives just like that.

Asher gave her hand a squeeze, and she could see that he understood everything she was feeling; she didn't have to explain, didn't have to say a word. He'd been there for it all. The constant disappointment. The visitations that had gone horribly wrong. Showing up at Katie's apartment high on God knew what, begging for money and leaving Katie a shell of herself. She'd call Asher, sobbing, and he'd come over and just hold her and talk it out with her, and she'd be okay. Until the next time, sometimes years in between. But she hadn't seen her mother in over three years until today. Before she'd had to flee Bear Ridge, Katie had tried to track her mother down, not to see her, but just to find out where she was, make sure she was at least alive. She'd been unable to locate her, though. While she'd been in hiding, Katie hadn't tried to find her mother through internet searches since she'd be unable to do anything with any information she'd found. She'd just tried to put it all out of her mind.

"Let's get you home," he said. "You and the twins could both use a nap."

He took her hand and helped her up and oh, how she wanted to just fall against him, feel his strong, muscular arms around her. But that had gotten her into trouble yesterday.

That afternoon, Asher was in his bedroom, packing for his wedding. All the details had been taken care of, so packing his suit and whatever else he needed for a day or two max was all that was left. His cousin Axel and his wife, Sadie, would be caretaking the ranch for him, their three-year-old and baby daughter their helper-elves.

He stared at the gray suit hanging in his closet, his one tie—he hated ties—on the hanger, wondering what Katie's dress looked like. And what he'd feel like seeing them all dressed up for the event.

He doubted she'd bought something white or poufy. She'd probably gone for understated, maybe even fancy but not a typical wedding dress. When they used to talk about getting married some-day—not to each other, of course—he'd tried to picture his faceless bride in a wedding gown, his bride walking down the aisle to where he'd be waiting, and for some reason he couldn't imagine it. Maybe he'd just lost interest or belief in that kind of big deal event because of his parents. His mother's second wedding cost a small fortune and she'd had two wedding gowns, one for the ceremony and one for the reception. His father's second wedding had also been that type of big wedding since it was the bride's first and she'd been sixteen years younger.

The longer he looked at the suit, the more he felt like he was already wearing it, the tie squeezing his neck. He wasn't sure why, though. His and Katie's wedding would be nothing like his parents' second weddings—or third, or his father's fourth—and there were no expectations to be squashed over the years. They *were* getting married for cause only.

Still, the marriage would be legal. And it was a big deal. It would be the two of them, married and sharing a home and a life and children. Neither would get romantically involved with other people for at least a year, as the will also stipulated the marriage last for the period of a year at minimum. The entire arrangement was kind of nutty and hard to think about but at least he would be going through it with his Katie. His best friend.

He wondered how she was doing right now. When they'd gotten home from the tribute, they'd skipped visiting the Christmas tree so that she could pick a wish request or two; she'd just wanted, needed to get home and process all that had happened with her mom. Since then, she'd been holed up with the twins in her room or the nursery and he could tell she wanted her space, some time to let everything sink in. They'd also talked about visiting the local animal shelter and seeing if there were any Australian shepherds or mixes, but that was probably better left to when they returned from the wedding since they wouldn't want to fall in love with a dog today and then have to leave for a couple days.

There was a knock at his door and he called, "Come in," and there she was, standing there looking troubled. Once again, it was all he could do not to grab her into his arms and just hold her like he usually would, like he always had after she'd had a bad run-in with her mom as a teenager or a young adult.

"I'm all packed," she said, her voice a bit strained. "How are you coming along? I know you hate packing."

"Still do," he said, upping his chin at the empty suitcase open on his bed. "I've got the suit and tie ready for the garment bag, so that's something."

She smiled, but it was a sad smile. Oh, Katie.

"Remember how I used to say I got through the hard experiences with my mother by imagining future good ones?" she asked. "Instead of being really sad about how high she was or a choice she'd made that broke my heart, I'd think to the future, about her being okay and helping me get ready on my wedding day, surprising me with something borrowed of hers, like a treasured pair of earrings."

"I do remember," he said, reaching out an arm to her shoulder. "I always thought that was really wise even if I couldn't manage it myself when it came to my own parents."

"Well, I guess I had nowhere to go but up. Hope got me through."

"I remember when we were seniors in high school and we heard she was sent back to prison for a year and a half, and you said something like that, 'One day she'll be a regular mom. Coming over for lunch to hear what's going on. Helping me get ready for my wedding. Babysitting for me. Just truly being there.'"

She nodded. "I clung to that. And now here she is, saying all that is possible. Well, maybe not helping me get ready for my wedding since that's tomorrow and I'm barely ready to *see* her again."

"Maybe it's enough that it's possible, you know? It means all that hope wasn't in vain. You had faith and you were right to."

Her pretty face brightened and she nodded slowly as if mulling that over. "I'm going with that. I'm not sure if I'd be a fool to trust her by even thinking she can stay clean for good, but time will tell, right?"

"Right."

She looked at him, her expression serious. "I have you, Asher. That's always been more than enough."

And then just like that, she was in his arms again, but it was his doing. He held her, resting his head lightly atop hers. He could feel her heart beat. He could smell her shampoo. And it was all back, those unexpected feelings he'd had yesterday in the attic.

Wanting her.

She was so close. She looked up at him, her pink-red plush lips so inviting and he leaned down slightly and kissed her, which sent blood coursing through every part of his body. She deepened the kiss to the point that there was no stepping back.

His hands were in her hair, on her sweater, moving under her sweater. He felt her hands snake around his neck, her lips on his neck. They tumbled onto the bed and he shoved off the empty suitcase.

It was only when the suitcase hit the floor with a thud that Asher froze, his hands slowly untwining from Katie's silky hair, his lips gone from hers. One minute he'd been lying on top of her, and now he was standing up, the air out of his lungs.

"I got caught in the moment," he whispered. "I'm sorry."

"*We* got caught up in the moment. And maybe the moment is a natural progression, Asher. It clearly is or we wouldn't be here...again, right?"

He shook his head. "A natural progression toward ruining things between us? Potentially destroying the family we're going to be? I can't do that."

She crossed her arms over her chest. Silent.

"We know how to be best friends, Katie. We know we're great at that. We had sex one night and didn't talk for a month. It made things complicated."

"*You* made things complicated," she said, standing up. "You. I was willing to see where things might go."

"The divorce rate—"

"I know plenty of couples who've been married for over twenty years," she interrupted. "Ash, your parents aren't the norm."

"They're what I know, what I experienced." He walked up to her and took both of her hands. "Five minutes ago you said you have me and it's always been enough. It's the same for me. And that's because we're safe. I don't want to jeopardize that. Especially because of the twins."

"So let me ask you this," she said. "Obviously, we're attracted to each other."

"Obviously," he agreed.

"So we're just going to ignore that while husband and wife, sharing a house and a life and the care of our children?"

"We've been best friends for twenty-five years. What's happening between us lately is just...novelty, I think. The shock of you being back. Us being parents together. It's Christmastime too. We'll fall into our old routine in no time."

She raised an eyebrow. "You think so?"

Relief hit him that she seemed to understand what he was saying, that he couldn't risk them.

"So we'll just forget that we almost ripped each other's clothes off just now?" she asked.

He looked at her—hard. She was beautiful in a way he hadn't quite noticed before. Sexy. Everything about her called to him. But as he'd just said, he chalked that up to the shock of them being back in each other's lives in a very big way.

Friendship was forever. Lust faded. Sometimes within a week. Between wives, his father once said he was madly in love and had met the woman of his dreams. Three days later, he didn't like the way she ate spaghetti or that she liked to shop a lot. A day after that, he'd met someone else. That kind of heady attraction couldn't be trusted. What he and Katie had built over twenty-five years could be.

"I'll finish packing for the twins," she said. "I have no idea what they should wear for the ceremony but I guess they should just be comfortable."

"*Comfortable* is everything," he said.

She tilted her head and then gave him something of a smile and left.

He dropped down on his bed, staring at the suitcase, his head jumbled. He'd done the right thing by stopping them from ripping those clothes off. He was 100 percent sure.

He just didn't know what he'd do with all that attraction to her, all that desire.

Chapter Nine

The Reiki and Crystal Healing Day Spa was housed in what looked like a small luxe log cabin–type lodge with a steeply pitched triangular roof and hunter green trim. It was close to the center of town, but at the tail end of a road where the property abutted a nature preserve. Mandy had inherited the building, which also included their attached three-bedroom home, and five acres of land from her late father, who'd run a hiking guide business from the lodge. Cherrywood, Wyoming, got a lot of tourists for the famed hot spring in town and Mandy's loyal clients gave her such good reviews that she'd gotten on the map a bit.

Katie definitely needed some crystal therapy, not that she knew very much about it. Last November, at the gathering at the ranch house after Cassie Dawson's funeral, Mandy had explained briefly that crystals had all kinds of healing properties and could have positive, lovely effects on the heart, mind, soul and body. Katie didn't know much about Reiki but was pretty sure it had to do with foot massage. Or something like that.

As Asher pulled into the crowded, though granted, not that large, parking lot, Katie could see the tension on his face. She'd been seeing that a lot lately. Like last night.

He could use some crystal therapy. And a foot massage.

Last night, she'd been upset at first when she'd left his room for her own, but then realized what was important to keep in mind was that he clearly wanted her. Asher Dawson was physically attracted to her when he hadn't been for years. *That* she could work with. Him shutting it down, shutting them down, she could work *on* that.

He put the car in Park and stared straight ahead for a moment as if trying to gear up for what lay ahead. Likely it was the combination of this weekend of his father, the marital issues *and* their wedding that had him so quiet. And last night too.

The door opened and a group of women came

out, followed by Mandy and John Dawson. Mandy hugged each woman, and off they went.

"Looks like they do a good business," Katie said.

The Dawsons waved and headed over to the pickup. Asher finally took his keys from the ignition.

"Ready or not," he said.

Katie smiled. "It's gonna be fine. We're doing a good thing by them and a good thing for us."

He looked at her and nodded, then gave her a smile, and she felt like he was somewhat back. "You're right. And for the twins."

"And for the twins," she agreed.

He opened the door and hopped out, the Dawsons each giving him a hug. His dad came over to Katie's side and opened the door for her.

"I can't wait to meet my grandsons," John said.

"Me too!" Mandy exclaimed. "I'm so excited!" Katie and Mandy had had a great video call yesterday afternoon and discussed what Katie and Asher had in mind for the wedding. Katie really didn't know what Asher wanted, but she assumed he wanted to keep it *very* simple. Mandy had said since it was just going to be the six of them, they could hone the details today.

Katie smiled and stepped out. "It's so nice to see you, Mandy."

Mandy was tall like her husband, at least five-ten in flat boots, and slender, with long, wavy honey-brown hair shot with the occasional silver strand and such warm hazel eyes. She wore a long puffy mauve coat that zippered asymmetrically. "Oh my goodness, you're the one it's nice to see." She threw her arms around Katie and held her tight for a moment. "I am so glad you're okay and back with us. I know I said that three times yesterday on our video call but I'm just so relieved and happy."

Katie smiled. Mandy was such a friendly person. And Katie had always liked John Dawson, even if he was on the self-absorbed side, which had been the case since Katie had met him. He just thought of himself first and never seemed to put much stock into how others felt. Surely Mandy, an empath and an intuitive person, had spotted these traits right away while they were dating. They'd had a whirlwind courtship, so perhaps Mandy had been too in love to pay attention to red flags. Or maybe they hadn't seemed like red flags at the time.

Relationships were complicated.

Asher took out Declan and handed the carrier to his dad, then got out Dylan.

"Well, look at that!" John exclaimed. "They look just like you, Asher."

"I definitely see Katie in those sweet, beautiful little faces too," Mandy added.

Hmm, Katie thought. The couple seemed all right. Not sniping at each other. No daggers being thrown.

"I'm so thrilled you're all here and that you're having your wedding at the spa," Mandy said as they headed up the porch steps.

"Not that you put much stock in vows," John muttered suddenly, eyeing his wife.

Uh-oh. Katie glanced at Asher and could see him slightly shaking his head.

"John, we said we wouldn't discuss our issues," Mandy whispered harshly as she led the way to the left and around the side of the building. "This is about Asher and Katie and their big day."

John frowned. "Well, it's hard to pretend nothing's wrong when you barely spoke a word to me since getting back this morning after you were gone for days. I'm trying here!"

"*Are* you?" Mandy asked. She opened a side door and led the way inside.

"Humph," John snapped and headed into the kitchen. "I made coffee if anyone needs. I sure do."

"I would love coffee," Katie said.

"Ditto," Asher said.

"And I would love to hold each of these adorable babies," Mandy said.

The moment Asher set the carriers on the edge of the rug by the big kitchen window, Mandy scooped up a baby. She snuggled Declan against her chest, giving his head a kiss.

"Oh, he smells so good!" Mandy said.

Katie smiled. "I never get tired of that baby shampoo scent."

"Same," Asher said as his dad handed him a mug of coffee and then poured two more.

"Now let me properly greet your twin brother." Mandy handed Declan to John. She kneeled down to pick up Dylan.

John's eyes misted. "Oh my. It's one thing to know you have a grandson. It's another to actually hold him. Oh wow," he whispered, looking down at the baby nestled in his arms.

"They're so beautiful," Mandy said, giving Dylan a nuzzle on his brown hair.

"That box over there is for the twins," John said, sitting down carefully with Declan snuggled against him. "I called Mandy yesterday and got her approval after seeing something real cute in the gift shop in town. It's from the two of us."

Katie glanced at Mandy and the woman's face had softened, so score one for John. It was smart of him to call her for her opinion and to include her in the gift, despite them having problems right now. That was thoughtful.

Katie grinned and picked up the big box wrapped with baby blue paper. She gave it a little shake. "What could it be?"

"Just a little something for the boys for the wedding," John said. "I saw it and thought, *Now isn't that the cutest darn thing.*"

Katie sat down at the table and ripped off the paper, smiling up at Asher, then lifting the lid off the box. Inside were two fleece tuxedo pj's. "Okay, now I'm gonna cry. These are perfect and adorable. How kind of you both to find a way to dress them up for the ceremony."

John grinned. "You're welcome."

"I can't wait to see them in them," Mandy said. "Katie, would you like a tour of the house and spa? Asher's been here a few times. Plus we can chat about tomorrow and more of what you envision."

Katie smiled. "Sounds great."

Mandy handed Dylan over to Asher. Katie looked at the two Dawson men, sitting there each with a baby, each looking so…rapt, that Katie's heart gave a little leap. This weekend was going to be great for father and son—Katie could feel it.

"This of course is the kitchen," Mandy said, heading out. "And this is the living room."

Katie glanced around. Decorated in soothing earth tones, the place was so welcoming. There was a grand stone fireplace and a wall of windows facing the backyard and all the land beyond it.

"Our bedroom is on this level," Mandy said,

pointing to a door down a short hall. "And up-stairs," she added, heading to the staircase, "are two bedrooms and a big bathroom with a great claw-foot tub. I have a great selection of bath beads. Help yourself to anything."

"Thanks, Mandy. I'm so glad we're all here."

"Me too." She led the way down the hall to a door and opened it. "Here's the guest room for you and Asher. There's a smaller room across the hall for the twins. You're sure you don't need anything for them? I can call a few mom friends to borrow just about anything you might need."

"I brought everything. The bassinets are fold-able. And though they're tiny humans, they do have a lot of stuff to cart around, but I've got it all."

"Then let me show you a couple of spots where I envision the ceremony and what I have planned for the vows. You can let me know if you want to go more simple or add anything on your own."

Vows. Katie hadn't thought about that beyond the basic ones she'd always heard in movies and TV shows and a few friends' weddings.

They went back downstairs. Mandy stopped in the arched living room doorway. "Here's one possibility. It's a lovely room and that fireplace is such a showpiece as is the view of the preserve and mountains beyond it. Or," she said, heading down the hall and opening a door with a wooden painted sign that read SPA above the doorframe, "this. The meditation room has the same view of the preserve and mountains and it's my favorite room of anywhere I've ever been."

The moment Katie walked into the space she knew this was where she wanted to have the ceremony. The walls were an eggshell blue and held many interesting paintings and drawings, white filmy curtains were on the windows and a huge jute rug was on the floor. The room was so peaceful and somehow mystical. And the view was spectacular.

"This is the place," Katie said.

"I had a feeling. So should we go grab Asher to discuss the vows?" Mandy asked. She touched the yellow-orange crystal star hanging from a pendant around her neck. She bit her lip and suddenly looked sad, then seemed to catch herself and smiled.

"John opened up a bit the other day about the two of you having some issues," Katie said. "I wanted to be honest about that. It's kind enough that you're officiating the wedding amidst some trouble in paradise. You don't need to deal with writing the vows. The standard vows are fine. It's the 'I Do's we want to say."

Which was true. Lingering on the ceremony would only hurt.

"I don't want to heap our problems on you at

such a joyous time, Katie. But to be honest, I'm
not sure I can take much more of John's lack of
consideration. I work hard at communicating, at
trying to understand where he's coming from, but
he just doesn't hear me. He doesn't see anything
as a problem. Because it's not…for him."

Katie nodded. "Well, it's clear that he loves
you very much and that this marriage means everything to him. So he'll just *have* to hear you if
he wants what he wants."

"But if it means everything, why isn't he trying?" Mandy asked. "That's what I don't get."

Katie certainly understood that. It was her
big question too where she and Asher were concerned.

That both she and Mandy had their work cut
out for them with the two Dawson men made her
feel a little better, a little less alone. She had high
hopes for this weekend.

For both couples.

While his dad watched the twins, Asher had
gone out to the car and brought in all their stuff.
The nursery was now set up with the folding bassinets and there was a diaper station upstairs and
downstairs. Declan and Dylan had started yawn-
ing and rubbing their eyes, so although Grandpa
didn't want to let go of either of them, they'd taken
the boys upstairs to put them down for a nap.

"So have you and Mandy talked more about the two of you?" Asher asked as they went back into the kitchen, Asher pouring refills on the coffee.

"I tried to, but all she did was quiz me on what crystals mean what," John said, wrapping his hands around his mug. "No, I don't know what amethyst does or which crystal is mood enhancing. I'm the accountant, not the practitioner."

"Well, Dad, maybe it bothers Mandy that you don't know anything about her business—*your* business. If crystals and their healing properties are her passion, shouldn't you take an interest? If I'm not mistaken, you mentioned that Mandy watches all the big games with you and keeps the snacks coming."

John seemed to be taking that in. "She does, that's true. I don't think she cares all that much about sports."

"Exactly. So learn what amethysts do."

"Huh," his dad said, sipping his coffee. "That *would* make her happy, if I knew more."

"Then do it."

"The gift shop in the spa lobby sells a book on the healing powers of crystals. I think I'll go buy one and read up when Mandy doesn't see. I'll surprise her."

"Good idea, Dad."

His dad's mood improved, Asher looked out the window to see Katie and Mandy in the yard, deep in conversation. About the wedding, most likely. Or the state of Mandy and John's marriage.

This time tomorrow there would be another marriage in the family. Asher wondered if in a month, he'd be asking his dad's advice on the subject—from the perspective of things being rocky. Katie seemed to want to see where things went. But that meant giving in to the wild attraction he felt for her. And that attraction plus the depth of his feelings for her was a dangerous combination. They'd end up where his dad and Mandy were. Arguing, Sniping. They might not even make it till the year term was up for the will. And he'd lose everything—his best friend, the ranch and being with the twins all the time.

But he was well aware that it was kind of crazy to deny his attraction to his wife in the name of saving their relationship and marriage. He and Katie would be sharing a room tonight. He'd seen the guest room. Not very big. With a king-size bed dominating the space. *And* his mind right now.

How in the heck were he and Katie going to make this all work? She seemed very optimistic about it all. But Asher was tied up in knots.

Maybe not getting it—this thing called love— just ran in the family.

Chapter Ten

"How many times have we shared a bed or a tent?" Asher asked that night as he came out of the attached bathroom where he'd gone to change into his pj's. A sexier-than-he-probably-realized navy T-shirt and low-slung Wyoming Cowboys sweatpants. "Probably a hundred times since we were little kids."

Katie tried not to ogle him from where she was sitting up against the headboard of the beautiful four-poster bed in their room, rubbing heavenly scented massage oil onto her legs. According to the description on the tray in the spa gift shop, the oil was infused with aphrodisiac elements. Mandy had come over and grinned when she saw what Katie was looking at and had said, *Oh, you definitely want some of that. Not that you love-birds need any help, I'm sure, but one inhalation of the blend of oils and oh my. Did I mention it warms to the touch too?*

Katie purchased three bottles.

Until last year, when things had gotten weird between them, Asher would strip right in front of her without a thought. To change clothes after working on the ranch or to go skinny-dipping. She could have been any male locker room buddy of his for how uninhibited he was. Katie had stripped down herself more than a few times, pur-posefully, slowly, lifting up her shirt, unhooking her bra. She all but put on Marvin Gaye's sexi-est song to accompany. Had he noticed? Had his gaze lingered on her breasts, which granted, were a basic B cup? Nope. He'd barely looked in her direction. Of course, Asher was a gentleman and wouldn't stare anyway. But of the two extremes, staring and complete lack of interest, Asher fell to the latter.

Right now? Different story altogether. He hadn't whipped off his clothes to change into his pajamas in front of her. Even if he was trying to remind himself that they were buddies and had been for-ever. He was trying to make tonight, sharing a room, a bed, no big whoop.

But his blue eyes were fastened to where her

hands were massaging her legs. And since Mandy had given her and Asher complementary spa robes, which ended midthigh, she was showing a lot of leg.

Oh, and since pregnancy, the B cup had morphed into a D.

Earlier, when she'd excused herself to take Gigi's call, Katie had asked her friend if it was wrong to play dirty, to try to entice Asher when he'd made it clear he wanted a platonic relationship and marriage. Katie had thought long and hard about it and just wasn't sure. Denying their attraction to avoid a potential risk felt wrong. As wrong as not respecting Asher's feelings to do exactly that.

Gigi didn't think anything was wrong with Asher being given the opportunity to explore his thoughts on the subject. If the scent of massage oil and the sight of Katie sensuously rubbing it onto her legs and arms got him all hot and bothered, well, then maybe, Gigi had said, he'd have to accept that ignoring his attraction to her wasn't going to work. Maybe he'd have to give in to it. And maybe he'd have to open his heart, mind and soul to a real marriage. Risk and all.

The way Gigi had put it, Katie would be doing her groom a *favor*.

So she continued massaging the oil onto her leg, stretching it out.

"I have a good idea for what we can do tonight," he said, sitting on the edge of the bed and then springing up. "Be right back."

Katie smiled and leaned back, putting the massage oil down. She slightly opened her robe at the cleavage area, making it look like it was simply draped that way. Then she waited. She knew he wasn't going to suddenly return naked with a stem of grapes between his teeth. But *maybe*. She giggled at the thought.

He was back. With his hands full.

"I knew I saw board games in the living room," he said. "I found Scrabble, Life, Monopoly. Even Battleship. I used to love that game when I was a kid."

Katie stared at the boxes stacked in his arms. And inwardly sighed.

"That lotion smells really good," he said. Brightly. Cheerfully. "So how about Scrabble first. Then Battleship."

Katie tightened the belt of her robe. Scrabble could be sexy, couldn't it? She was really good at all word games, and smart was hot. Plus, playing in bed could lead to him writing out words on her body with his fingertip. You never knew.

He got up with the Scrabble box and set it on the

round café table by the window, then sat down—
as far from the bed as he could get in the room.
"I'll turn over the tiles."

Katie inwardly sighed again.

"Exqueeze me?" Asher heard Mandy screech
from downstairs.

He glanced at Katie beside him in bed. Her
eyes widened. It was just after midnight, and he
and Katie had just gotten into bed after quite a
few board games and stalling on his part. They'd
had tea and a midnight snack downstairs. They'd
talked about how they might divvy up the ranch
chores when they got home, who would do what
and when. He'd taken notes at the table. Anything
to avoid getting into that big bed in the small
room. But finally he couldn't help the yawn, then
realized that would work in his favor. He'd probably be asleep in under two minutes. No time to
notice Katie sensuously massaging oil onto her
long, shapely legs again. On her arms. He'd barely
been able to handle the delicious scent. Sandal-
wood, definitely. Lavender, he was pretty sure.
Thank the Lord she'd changed out of that short,
sexy robe and into pj's—and not in front of him.

"Exqueeze me is never a good sign," Katie said,
sitting up.

"Nope," he agreed. "Did we bring earplugs?"

She shook her head. "Wish we did."

There was no response from his dad, so Asher figured they were either whispering downstairs or his father was trying to come up with a response to whatever had gotten Mandy's goat—no pun intended.

"Well, I was reading up on the healing properties of citrine," his dad finally said, "and you wear that citrine star necklace every day. It's supposed to protect you from negative energy but..."

Katie grimaced. "Oooh," she said, shaking her head slowly.

"But what?" Mandy asked, impatience tinging her voice.

"Well, I just thought maybe it's not working," John said. "You could try a different crystal that's mood enhancing."

Silence for a moment. Then: "You can go sleep on the sofa, John Dawson," Mandy muttered.

There was a thumping sound, like a pillow hitting the wall.

Asher shook his head. "This thing with the crystals and his lack of interest—until just recently—in something so important to Mandy reminds me of how he always felt about the goat ranch. He didn't like having to do barn chores as a kid, had no interest in ever taking over the ranch or helping with the dairy business. How could he not take an interest in the biggest thing in his world at whatever moment?"

"Well, he's trying now. And numbers are his thing and they always were," Katie pointed out. John's accounting business in Brewster was booming and he handled all the financials for the spa.

"I guess. I don't know what I'm saying. I'm not one to look for deeper meaning—maybe being here at the spa is rubbing off on me."

Katie smiled. "Not a bad thing at all."

"Some things just have to be accepted at face value, I think."

Katie turned to look at him, propping up on an elbow. "What I don't get is where the change between them happened. *When* it happened. How different could your dad have been a year ago? What's causing the friction? It's like Mandy is suddenly noticing certain aspects to his personality."

He lay in the same position facing her, on his side, propped on an elbow. "She was blinded by being madly in love. She told me so when I met her for the first time. That she was madly in love. That's never gonna work out."

"Asher. That's so cynical. People fall madly in love all the time and get married and celebrate their silver and golden anniversaries."

A lock of her silky brown hair fell into her

face, and he tucked it behind her ear, so aware of touching her, wanting to linger on her cheek, her ear, wanting to kiss her.

"Well, maybe if people married for solid reasons," he said, "like a great friendship and a true life partner, there would be less friction. Less divorce. Fewer families being ripped apart."

Great friendships were not built on kisses. Or on how badly he wanted her.

She raised an eyebrow. "I think most people have very good intentions when they marry."

"We definitely do. I've never been so sure that we're headed down the right path. A platonic marriage."

She tilted her head. "For a year, you mean. Until the will stipulation is satisfied."

"No," he said. And as the word echoed in his head, he shifted back a bit. Then a bit more. Putting some space between them. "Forever. I take this seriously, Katie. I take the vows seriously. It's why I got so tied in knots last year and ruined everything."

"We're thirty, Asher. You're saying you're not going to have sex for the next fifty years?"

He dropped onto his back and stared up at the ceiling. "Fine, that sounds insane. We'll take it one step at a time. I just know that the madly-in-love nonsense and lust fade over time. If a couple is lucky, they're best friends and their relationship is strengthened by their history and commitment. My dad—not lucky. And this is the fourth time. So forget about being lucky. It's about being wise. Knowing the difference between what's real and what's a fantasy you've created about someone."

"You're being way too hard on love in all its many forms—fast or slow."

He turned to face her again. "I just want to protect what we have. Not just for us, Katie, but for the twins. Last week in the diner, a couple I know who meet in the parking lot to drop off their baby for the weekend custody arrangement were screaming at each other. What happens when that baby is old enough to understand?"

"I hear what you're saying, but giving up on love—the real thing—is not the answer. Giving up on attraction and lust isn't the answer either."

"What is the answer?" he asked.

"It's what you said. Taking it step by step. Feeling things out. Not making grand statements against the most fundamental thing in the universe."

"I just want things to be great for us and the twins, Katie. That's all."

"I know," she said, reaching out to touch his cheek. "I do too. Our first step just happens to be marriage. We'll see what happens when we get back home into everyday life."

"I've been thinking," he said. "I know we talked

about maybe staying here again tomorrow night, but I like the idea of starting our married life at home. At the ranch." He took her hand and held it, looking into her eyes.

Home. More than anyone, Asher knew what that word meant to her. It was everything. From age four until she turned eighteen, she'd lived in two different group homes, and though he knew she'd had an okay experience in both and had made a few friends who'd even felt like family over the years, the relationships had been transient as kids were adopted or the state had found relatives who'd taken them in. Asher had helped her move into a couple of apartments in town, but despite finally having a home of her own, she hadn't liked living alone. She'd always said that he was her home. Him and the Dawson Sweet Dairy Ranch.

And now it really was home. He was glad to be able to give her that.

"I think that sounds perfect," she said, and he could tell she was touched.

"And this way, my dad and Mandy can get some needed time alone with a wedding and grandparent time under their belts." He'd already had his fill of his father and his lack of understanding about people and thinking about others and their feelings. Such as his wife's.

"I really think they're gonna be fine," Katie

said. "A rough patch right now is all. And getting over and through it will make their marriage stronger."

"Or they'll divorce," he said.

"Nah. They love each other. I can see that without knowing either of them well."

He had no idea if they'd weather through. His dad's previous three marriages hadn't lasted. Why would this one when it was on thin ice so fast? But Katie really seemed to think so and right now, he could use a dose of her faith in people.

He nodded but his head still felt so jumbled about this. "I don't know what I'd do without you." He shook his head. "Actually I do know. I found out for a year. And it was the worst year of my life."

"We're gonna be okay. Just trust in us."

He heard another thud and realized it was the sound of the pull-out sofa opening.

He just didn't want *that* to be in his future.

Chapter Eleven

Since Mandy and John would be working most of Saturday, the busiest day at the spa, Mandy had invited Katie and Asher to a wedding breakfast pre-opening. The four adults and two babies sat around the table in the dining room, which was laden with French toast sprinkled with powdered sugar and cinnamon, a platter of bacon, fresh fruit, mimosas and lots of coffee. Katie was on her second cup.

"We really appreciate that you two watched the twins for us last night," Katie said. They'd moved the bassinets into the living room, and the Dawsons had kept their door open so they could hear any fussing or crying, which was why their voices had carried up the stairs last night.

Asher nodded, forking a slice of French toast onto his plate and then drizzling it with maple syrup. "I've only been a dad a very short time so I actually still like leaping out of bed in the middle of the night to take care of a shrieking baby, but that probably won't last."

John smiled. "Definitely not. I was a leaper, you know. You'd cry as an infant, and I'd race into the nursery to see if you were choking—on what, I have no idea since there wasn't anything but you in the crib."

Asher stared at his father. "I didn't know you did night duty when I was a baby."

Katie was surprised too. John Dawson hadn't been a doting dad according to Asher—or from what Katie had seen over the years. Once Asher's mom and John had separated when Asher was young, he'd have every other weekend visits and they alternated holidays.

"Well, Asher's mother and I decided we'd take turns but I'd always get up anyway. There's just something about your tiny baby needing you in the middle of the night."

"Aww," Mandy said, her gaze soft on her husband. "I know what you mean. When Daphne was a baby I felt that way." Katie knew it was hard on Mandy that her daughter and two grandchildren lived far away in California, but they visited several times a year.

John took a sip of his mimosa. "I'd get to the office all bleary-eyed—not a good look for an accountant, but that's what double espressos are for."

"Definitely," Katie said.

Asher seemed about to say something but clearly thought better of it, and it was probably a good idea. Or maybe not. She could imagine him saying something like she'd been thinking, that he sure hadn't been around much for a dad who raced into the nursery to make sure his baby was still breathing. But sometimes it was better to sit with surprising new information rather than come back with a dig about the past—and present.

Baby steps applied to Asher and John's relationship too.

"You know," Mandy said, biting her lip, "last night, John and I were squabbling and to be honest, he even slept on the couch—"

"Don't remind me," John said, rubbing his back with one hand and taking a piece of bacon with the other.

"But when I woke up this morning, so aware that it was your wedding day," Mandy continued, looking from Katie to Asher and then at her husband, "all I could think about was *our* wedding day."

Katie smiled. "What was your wedding like?"

"We eloped to Las Vegas," John said. "Katie's a big Elvis Presley fan and we got married by a terrible impersonator but boy, did we laugh."

Mandy laughed now too. "He was terrible. He looked nothing like Elvis, first of all, and had the most exaggerated mannerisms. His lip quirked up to his cheeks, and with every word he said, he'd cock a hip, then roll his hips. John and I were in hysterics while repeating our vows."

Asher smiled and forked a bite of French toast. "That does sound fun."

"Then we went back to our hotel. John booked us the most over-the-top honeymoon suite with a heart-shaped jet spa and mirrors everywhere and we listened to Elvis's most romantic songs while having a wedding feast on the balcony, just the two of us. It was so romantic. We even had a mini wedding cake. And lots of champagne. It was a dream."

John paused with a forkful of French toast halfway to his mouth and then put it down. "It was a great time," he said with a nod, glancing out the window and biting his lip.

Katie could tell he was lost in a memory. Mandy was looking at her husband with the most wistful expression.

"Was it love at first sight?" Katie asked, thinking this track of good remembrances would be helpful. "When you met? How did you meet, anyway?"

"It was for me," John said, then took a sip of his mimosa. "I met Katie in the park in Bear Ridge where I'd gone to eat my lunch because it was a gorgeous October day. And I saw a woman trying to entice a stray dog out from under a bench. She had treats and a dog toy and I thought it must be her dog, but it turned out to be a stray—filthy and injured and scared. Mandy had seen it and had called the animal warden but the dog took off like a shot when the man arrived. The second he left, the dog came back and ran under the bench, so Mandy went to get some supplies to lure him out. I met her when she was holding out a treat and saying, 'Come on out, sweetie pooh, I want to help you.'"

"Aww," Katie said, looking from John to Mandy. "I didn't know this story."

"Me either," Asher said, taking another slice of French toast. "Did the dog come out?"

"Well, that's where I came in," John said. "I thought this woman trying to help this dirty, skinny dog had to be a kind and patient soul, and I just fell in love with her right there. Ash," he added, turning to his son, "you know the story of my childhood dog, Biscuit, how I found him as a stray and my parents finally relented to my whining and let me bring him home. Then just a few months later, he was hit by a speeding car and I couldn't handle the idea of ever having a dog again. So when I saw her being so kind to that stray dog under the bench, that was it. Mandy was faced away from me at first so I didn't even know what she looked like."

Asher stared at his father, a piece of bacon paused in the air. "Love at first sight because of *what* she was doing rather than what she *looked* like—that may be a first."

"I'll be honest," Mandy said. "It was love at first sight for me because he was so damned handsome *and* because he came over to help, knowing to stay at a distance because the dog was clearly afraid of men."

"I adore this story," Katie said.

"Happy ending for the dog?" Asher asked, finally eating his bacon.

"Well," Mandy continued, "your dad stuck around for *two* hours until the dog came out and I could get a leash on him. We brought him over to the vet to check for a microchip and it turned out he belonged to a family a town over and he'd been missing for two weeks. Poor thing. When we dropped him off at their house, a little boy came running out sobbing and threw his arms around the dog, whose name was French Fry."

"Even I started crying," John said.

Mandy gave her husband a warm smile. "And

that's when I knew I'd met the man I was going to marry."

"We were inseparable from that moment on," John said. "And a week later, I proposed. Sure, sounds a little fast. But when you're in your late fifties and have been through a thing or two, you know what you know. And I *knew*."

Katie let out a happy sigh. "So romantic and sweet."

"Come help me make another pot of coffee," Mandy said to John with a soft smile.

"Anything, my love," John said, popping up.

Katie watched the couple head into the kitchen. She could just see them in an embrace at the far end. Her heart soared. "Ash," she whispered, nodding toward the kitchen.

"They probably should have dated longer before making that kind of lifelong commitment," Asher whispered. "Mandy wouldn't have been so fast to discount or dismiss the things that would bother her later. Like now."

"What matters is *that*," she whispered back, gesturing at the couple, who were standing with their arms around each other, whispering and staring into each other's eyes. "The strength of their love for each other. They can get through these issues that come up because of that deep core. They'll always remember it, as they did just now."

Asher drained his coffee. "So Mandy's just

going to ignore that John doesn't give two figs about which crystal is which?"

"Maybe she'll decide that it's not a deal breaker, after all. Maybe she'll decide other things about him are more important and that she has to overlook a few things that bug her. No couple can possibly love everything about each other."

"Talk about learning to communicate after the fact," Asher said.

"That's okay. We're starting from home base because we're best buds. But there's a lot we'll still have to learn about each other as a married couple."

He looked at her as if she'd grown another head. "I know everything about you. You know everything about me."

Katie smiled and shook her head. "As *friends*. But now we'll be married. That adds a whole new dimension. And we're parents. That's also new."

"But the basics are there. I know who you are, Katie Crosby. And I love that person. So that's where we're starting from. Love and friendship for twenty-five years."

Katie felt her heart give another little leap. Of course, she'd always known that he loved her—as a friend. But add in the attraction he was trying to squash and ignore and that meant they had moved on to a new plane. Where love and attraction would take their relationship to a marriage in every sense of the word.

"I love you too, Asher," she said, then felt her cheeks heat. She'd said that a hundred times over the years for this or that reason. But never under these circumstances.

Mandy and John came into the dining room just then with the refilled carafe of coffee.

"I could definitely use another cup of that," Asher said fast.

He loved her. She knew that. Talk about starting on home base.

After breakfast, Mandy and John headed to the spa—John worked the front desk on Saturdays since they'd discovered their customers liked the family aspect to the business and how John fawned and fussed over them, offering infused water and herbal tea and falling over himself to be helpful. The lobby was also the gift shop and had an enchanting quality to it, Katie thought as she looked around. The pale blue walls held paintings and drawings and tapestries, and there were many display cases of essential oils and crystals and incense.

"How helpful can my dad be when he can't answer a single question about the treatments the spa offers?" Asher whispered as they browsed the display of healing crystals for sale, the twins napping in their double stroller in a corner.

A woman and her daughter came in just then and checked in for their crystal healing massages, asking John the difference between moonstone and tiger's eye for motivation.

"Well, let's look through the *Reiki and Crystal Healing Day Spa's Free Guide to Healing Crystals*, written by Mandy Dawson, expert in crystals, which you can take home with you." John grabbed two of the pamphlets and flipped through, reading the descriptions of moonstone and tiger's eye. "And of course, Delilah, your practitioner for your treatments, will go further in detail and answer any questions you may have."

The women were all smiles as they said yes to herbal teas, which John got busy making at the refreshment credenza.

Katie and Asher took a pamphlet and were reading through it when Asher said, "Moonstone. That's the one for us."

Katie glanced at the photo of the beautiful clearish-white crystal and read the description. "'Moonstone will illuminate your path, like the moon itself, and provide insight to emotions while helping you stay centered.'

"Perfect," she said. Maybe it wasn't focused on love and marriage and the heart like some others, like rose quartz, but it was spot-on for their needs. They picked two from the display case, one smooth and one more roughly cut, and of course John refused to take their money.

Then all that was left to do was relax and enjoy the day. They took a walk toward the mountain, then drove into the bustling tourist town to window-shop with the twins in their stroller. The weather wasn't too bad for December in Wyoming, and two mugs of hot cocoa in a coffee shop where they'd stopped to feed the twins had hit the spot.

By three, it was time to head back to the spa to prepare for the wedding, not that it would take Katie all that long to get ready. She had her dress and shoes. She'd wear a little makeup and leave her hair loose, a seed-pearl headband that Gigi had given her adding a bridal touch. And she had the gold bracelet her father had left her. She'd really only need an hour to shower and get ready. Mandy had offered to close the spa for the afternoon to help Katie prepare, but Katie had said absolutely not. She'd almost added, *not for a sham wedding.*

But it wasn't a sham wedding. The marriage would be legal. And very real.

Maybe it wasn't what she'd envisioned when she'd dreamed about her wedding day as a girl. When she'd fantasized, often, as a full-grown woman, about marrying Asher Dawson. But this was what she had and she'd make the most of it and try with everything she had to show Asher there was no denying their relationship had shifted. She'd been attracted to him forever; his romantic feelings for her were new. Or finally unearthed.

And tonight would be their wedding night. Back at the ranch. Home.

Chapter Twelve

In the big beautiful meditation space, there was a small dressing room where Katie was getting ready with Mandy hovering nearby to lend a hand with a zipper or a clasp, and a large walk-in closet that was serving as Asher's dressing room, his dad sitting in the chair beside the standing mirror. The twins were napping in their double stroller beside John. Asher figured the babies would wake up any minute, and because the ceremony wouldn't be very long, he and Katie could get them changed and fed right afterward when they'd officially start their lives together as husband and wife. A family.

"I always knew you and Katie would end up together," John said.

Asher straightened his tie and glanced at his dad. "Why's that?"

"Inseparable from what, age five? Then you realized how much you loved her when you thought she was lost to you forever." John shook his head. "Thank God she's back. And what a gift those two little boys are, Ash."

Asher froze. If he wanted a better relationship with his father, maybe he should tell him the truth about him and Katie and why they were marrying. But John's words were echoing in his head. *Then you realized how much you loved her...*

"I've always loved Katie. That hasn't changed." At least he could inject some honesty.

"There's a big difference between loving a good friend and being in love, Ash. But I don't have to tell you that."

He looked at his dad, who had a moony expression in his blue eyes. Asher should just be grateful that things were better between his dad and Mandy. Asher liked Mandy, liked the two of them together. He'd been wary of his first stepmother for simply being next after Asher's mother. And his next stepmother wasn't very interested in getting to know Asher. But Mandy had been warm and friendly immediately.

Asher could remember being shocked when his

father had told him he was getting married again after his divorce from Asher's mother. There was so much tension between his parents, lots of arguing, often over stupid stuff, that Asher had been sure neither parent would ever want to live with someone again. But both had. His dad's second wife was a rodeo champ, a bull rider, and she was always on the road, and between that and the danger of her great passion, which remained the rodeo and not John Dawson, they'd started arguing too. Weekends that his dad had his visitation, teenage Asher would spend around the rodeo circuit. He'd thought his new stepmother was pretty cool and fearless, but that the marriage hadn't lasted more than two years wasn't a surprise to anyone. After their split, Asher had once again been sure his dad would swear off marriage forever. He'd been wrong. Again. His father had dated a lot of women afterward, some a few months, some lasting a year or two, and John Dawson had outright said he was looking earnestly for his next wife, that he loved being married.

Number three was a waitress at his dad's favorite diner in Brewster with three grown children, and after a year of constantly visiting them, John Dawson put his foot down about traveling to see people he didn't find very appealing. That marriage had lasted another year.

After their divorce, Asher had asked his dad
if he was done now, and his father had said of
course not. Asher had shaken his head, not getting it, not getting his father at all. He'd told his
dad to really get to know the next woman he got
serious about so that he didn't jump into another
problematic relationship. But his father had insisted it wasn't the relationships that were problematic, it was people and their complexity and
some got lucky with the dynamic over time, some
made it work and some just couldn't. One day,
his father had added, it'd work out forever, and
he and his wife would grow old on their porch
together. His father hadn't been daunted by his
divorces or turned off by marriage at all.

There'd been a long stretch when his father was
single, the past ten years or so. And then he'd met
Mandy, and Asher had been expecting more of
the same. They didn't seem to have anything in
common, but it was clear as he saw them together,
particularly this morning, that they truly loved
each other. And that maybe the marriage would
work out, after all. Then again, they were having
problems and they'd barely been married a year.

As if Asher was one to judge. His longest relationship had been a couple years—and that was
three years ago—but she'd given him an ultima-
tum to propose and he hadn't been able to. He'd
agonized for weeks with Katie over that relation-

ship, should he or shouldn't he, Katie trying to give him good advice without telling him outright what to do. Near the end, when the girlfriend said he had until the next day to propose or she was done, he'd asked Katie if he should just buy a ring and propose and marry her because he clearly did love her and was probably just nervous about marriage because of his parents' track records. Cold feet, cold heart.

Katie had said very seriously that Asher knew, deep down, what he wanted to do. If he wanted to marry that woman or not. *The answer is right here*, she'd said, reaching out a hand to touch his heart.

And he'd known in that instant that he didn't love that girlfriend, not in the way you were supposed to love the person you would marry.

But now, he was marrying Katie for practical reasons—important practical reasons. What was so strange was that marrying her felt right, despite the fact that they'd be platonic. He was marrying her for the right reasons because their kind of love, built from years of pure friendship, would last. And he was marrying for the twins, first and foremost, and then for their legacy: the ranch. He was marrying his best friend. Like his dad said.

"It's just before six," John said, eyeing his watch. "Ready?"

"Ready," Asher said, then cleared his throat.

He looked at himself in the mirror, at this groom-to-be in a suit he wore every couple of years. "To the start of everything," he added.

"Amen to that," his dad said, standing up and clapping Asher on the back.

John kneeled down in front of the stroller and ran a finger down the cheek of each sleeping baby. "Now you listen here, guys. Your daddy is getting married to your mama. Isn't that something? That the two of you and your mother are here is a miracle. And after everything the four of you have been through, separately and together, nothing could ever tear your family apart. Now, some may say that a man married four times has no business making any pronouncements about lasting love. But it just took me longer to know what I have. That's the key to marriage. Knowing what you have. Of course, both spouses have to know it. At the same time. I guess that's the hard part."

Asher stared at his father, wondering what the man had done with former caveman John Dawson. As his dad stood up and gave each boy a gentle caress on their brown hair, Asher smiled at his sons in their adorable tuxedo pj's. His father was responsible for that. And here the man was, getting Asher all emotional. About how close he felt to his dad right now when he hadn't felt that way in decades. Maybe ever.

"I'm glad you're here, Dad. I mean, I'm glad I'm here. That you're part of this."

His father's eyes got misty. "Me too. You have no idea."

He gave his dad a hug, neither of them too comfortable with this new mushy side to things, and they headed out, Asher pushing the stroller and his dad texting Mandy.

"They'll be out in a minute," John said, leading the way to the front of the room where they'd set up a small platform and hung white muslin and twinkling white lights, a table lined with pots of pink and red roses behind the podium. A long runner went from the back of the room to the plat-form. John and Mandy had created an aisle for Katie to walk down, he realized. His dad parked the stroller beside him, the twins just waking up.

Mandy came out, wiping away tears. "I'm al-ready crying and the ceremony hasn't even started. Katie looks so beautiful." She headed to the table and pressed something behind the pots of roses, and classical music began playing softly, then she moved behind the podium, picking up a small booklet in some kind of vellum.

Asher moved to his spot on the platform in front of the podium and stared at the door. Fi-nally, it opened and Katie stepped out, her gaze right on Asher. He swallowed. She did look beau-tiful. Stunning.

His breath caught in his throat and he froze for a second. *Your life partner is about to walk down the aisle to you. The mother of your children.* He let out the breath, unable to take his eyes off her. She was looking at him too, her expression containing so many emotions he couldn't pick any out.

His dad had his phone in hand to take photographs and video. Katie began walking down the aisle, her eyes never leaving Asher's, her expression serious yet she seemed to be blinking back tears. She joined him on the platform and reached out her hands, and he gently held them as he faced her.

"We are gathered here today to join Asher and Katie in matrimony," Mandy began. "To toast to love. Though I haven't known either of you very long, your love for each other is so strong and vital that it emanates from the two of you." She smiled at them both. "You may exchange rings now, and slide them down once you each say your vows."

The rings. They'd forgotten the rings.

Asher looked at Katie, then at Mandy. "Everything happened so fast that rings must have slipped our minds."

"There's a display of rings in the lobby," Katie said. "John, will you grab two plain silver bands?"

John dashed out and returned with the two

rings, which would do for now. But Asher would get them real wedding rings once they were back home.

Asher nodded at his father and took them, sliding one halfway down Katie's ring finger. She did the same with his.

She turned to Asher. "Asher, do you take this woman, Katie, to be your lawfully wedded wife, in sickness and in health, for richer and for poorer, till death do you part?"

"I do," Asher said, stuck on that last part. His father's words came back to him. *Inseparable from what, age five? Then you realized how much you loved her when you thought she was lost to you forever.*

This might not be a typical marriage, but Asher was going to make it work. Not for a year to meet the terms of the will. Forever. Whatever he had to do to never lose Katie again. *You just have to know what you have,* he recalled his father saying. And Asher knew. He absolutely knew what he had in Katie, in their future. But he knew Katie didn't think a platonic marriage was sustainable.

Hell, he didn't know either. How could it be? Especially when he wanted Katie so bad he'd had to lie very still last night when he'd woken up in the middle of the night. She'd been right beside him, on her stomach, an arm over his chest. Wearing some sexy tank top and yoga pants. He'd forced his eyes and thoughts off her and onto the ceiling, trying to make himself think about diapers and baby bottles and goats and fences. At some point, her hand had found his, though she seemed to still be asleep, and the comfort of it had actually lulled him to sleep. But if they nixed the platonic part, their marriage would be subject to all the problems that plagued other marriages. The focus would be on romantic love instead of partnership and friendship.

"And do you, Katie," Mandy said, "take Asher to be your lawfully wedded husband..."

As Mandy continued with the vows, Asher felt like time stopped and all he could hear was his own heartbeat and all he could see was Katie with her sweet freckles and her beautiful dress.

One day at a time, he told himself. Baby steps. They'd figure this out.

"The bride and groom may now kiss," Mandy said, then wiped tears from under her eyes.

He reached out his hands to both sides of her face and kissed her, then more deeply, though he hadn't meant to. She looked at him and kissed him back.

Mandy was clapping while John continued to point his phone at them. Capturing memories right now.

"Introducing Asher and Katie Dawson!" Mandy

shouted happily. "If you're taking his name. I shouldn't assume."

Katie laughed. "We actually talked about that. I'm going to be Katie Crosby Dawson in honor of my father and in honor of my marriage to my sons' father." She held Asher's hand and they walked over to the stroller, each taking a baby.

"What a beautiful, sweet ceremony," Mandy said.

"Agreed," John said, wiping tears. "I have a little something for the officiant," he added.

"For me?" Mandy asked, clearly surprised.

He reached into his pocket and held out his closed palm. Mandy pried open his fingers and brought her hand to her mouth.

"Oh, John."

"What is it?" Katie asked, stepping closer.

"It's a rough-hewn rose quartz," John explained. "It's considered the love stone and is about forgiveness and reconciliation. I love you, Mandy Dawson."

Mandy threw her arms around him. "I love you too. So much."

Asher glanced at Katie, whose eyes had gone all misty. "This wedding brought two couples together."

"Sure did," Mandy said, holding her husband's hand.

John held up his phone with his free hand and

swiped through the photos and videos. "Will you look at this?" he said, hitting Play on the video of the wedding kiss.

"Wow," Katie said, looking up at Asher.

Wow was right. That was some kiss. And there was nothing platonic about it.

There was a surprise waiting for them at the ranch. Asher had done some Christmas decorating already—just some lights around the door and the wreath on the barn—but now the house and trees were all decked out, with white lights across the roof and a beautiful wreath with a red ribbon on the front door. The evergreens near the house were festooned with multicolored lights. The ranch looked so festive and sparkly.

"Wow, do you think Axel and Sadie did this?" Katie asked, staring in wonder at how beautiful the place looked.

"I'm sure," Asher said. "Though I wouldn't be surprised if all my cousins had a hand in this." About a half hour ago, he'd texted Axel to let him know they were on their way, and his cousin had responded that the goats were taken care of for the night and that he, Sadie and his kids were headed home.

Katie stared at him and put her hand on his arm. "Asher, I just realized something. I've always wanted a big family, you know that. And now your cousins *are* my family." She grinned. "The twins sure are lucky to have those Dawsons around."

"And a grandmother," he said—gently, she noticed.

"Well, I won't hold my breath about that."

"Your mom looked healthy, Katie. And sounded strong and sure of herself. I have a good feeling."

Katie bit her lip and could barely shrug. "I've been here before, Asher. She looked healthy, yes, more so than I've ever seen her. But when have I ever been the catalyst for her to get her life together? It took until she thought I was dead? I'm not sure how I feel about that. Once again *I* didn't matter."

"I don't know about that, Katie. This is personal and I have no business telling you how to feel about your mother. I'm just asking you to keep an open mind."

Open mind, open heart. That had been the motto at her first group foster home. After a while, though, Katie had learned to stop hoping. She was never going to have a family, be adopted, because her mother had refused to sign away her rights. There had been those who'd thought that meant her mother loved her. But as Katie had gotten older, particularly into her teens, that little door she'd always kept open, hoping and praying her mother would either get clean and come for her or allow her to find a new family like so many of the kids who'd come through the home, had almost closed completely. By the time she'd reached adulthood and her mother had come only for money, the door had finally closed. But the pain always got in.

Don't think about this. It's Christmastime and this ranch is your home now. You're married to the man you love. You have everything you ever dreamed of.

She looked at Asher long and hard, loving every bit of his face. His long dark eyelashes. The sexy, thick, tousled hair. His blue eyes and strong jaw. As long as he was by her side, everything would always be okay.

"You all right?" he asked, peering at her.

"Definitely," she said with a smile.

He smiled back, and got out of the truck. She couldn't wait to go inside. The ranch had an all-new meaning to her now. Home.

As Asher carried in their bags and came back out to grab Dylan's carrier, Katie took out Declan and wondered if grooms still carried their brides over the threshold. Not with two baby carriers in their hands, she reminded herself, a grin forming. Theirs wasn't going to be a traditional marriage in every sense—the big one, of course—but in lots of ways, it would be. And Katie was going to make the most of it.

And show her husband just how wonderful a real marriage could be.

Tonight was their wedding night. It could go one of two ways. Sexless or the opposite.

And Katie was planning on the opposite.

Chapter Thirteen

Both babies were rubbing their eyes and fussing, so Asher and Katie hadn't even changed out of their wedding clothes before getting the twins ready for bed. Katie walked the nursery with Dylan, who'd been screeching a minute ago, snuggled in her arms, singing a lullaby, while he stood rocking Declan, whose little eyes were getting droopier and droopier. Every few seconds, the heavy eyes would slightly open and then close, and finally, Asher could tell Declan was asleep.

As he touched a kiss to both babies' heads in their bassinets, Asher figured he and Katie would go to their bedrooms to change into something a lot more comfortable when he realized that Katie might not want to.

"Notice the bucket of champagne and two glasses that Axel and Sadie left us on the coffee table?" he asked as they left the nursery.

"I sure did," she said with a smile. "We can have our own private wedding reception."

Or they could change into sweats, make some pasta, see what was on Netflix and just act like this was any old day. And night. Except it was their wedding night.

He could try to control this or he could just see what happened. On one hand, he liked the idea of where champagne and a wedding night would very naturally lead them. On the other, it was asking for trouble. If they made love tonight, then what? Would that mean they would share a bedroom? That their relationship would not be platonic going forward?

You don't have to have everything decided. Just be more like Katie and see where this leads. See what happens.

Downstairs, they stood behind the coffee table, Katie holding both glasses as Asher popped the cork on the champagne. He poured and they held their glasses up.

"To second chances," he said.

She stood so close. Clinking distance. She looked so beautiful. Like the Katie he'd always known and someone new at the same time. Someone whose brown eyes were suddenly sultry. Someone whose pink-red lips were drawing him even closer. Her perfume was intoxicating, something slightly spicy.

"And new beginnings," she added, holding his gaze.

He swallowed. "I will definitely toast to that."

They clinked glasses and each took a long sip. If the doorbell hadn't rung just then, he might have put both their glasses down and taken her hands and let these old-new people they were do what came naturally.

At the door was a man in a white chef's coat and hat with a silver cart laden with covered trays. "A wedding gift from Gigi Robertson," the man said.

Katie grinned. "I *am* starving."

"Me too."

The man wheeled in the cart and said to leave it outside tomorrow by noon and he'd be back for it.

Asher brought the cart over to the café table near the sliding glass doors to the deck. It was lightly snowing, and between the twinkling lights on the deck railing and the flurries, the backdrop seemed magical. "Let's see what we're having," he said, pulling up the lid on the large tray. His mouth watered as he looked down at two very delicious-looking filet mignons in a peppercorn sauce. Another silver platter held roasted potatoes and another asparagus. There was also another bottle of champagne.

"This is amazing," she said.

Almost too romantic, he was thinking but was glad he didn't say. It was romantic. And romance wasn't what he'd envisioned for this marriage, but Katie looked so happy. He wasn't about to ruin that with reminders no one needed.

They ate and talked and laughed and drank and reminisced, covering everything from happy childhood memories they shared to how adorable the twins had looked in their tuxedo onesies.

"I think your dad and Mandy are going to be okay," Katie said, taking a sip of her champagne.

"I think so too. They may even go the distance."

"Wow," she said. "That is actual optimism about their marriage. I'm impressed."

"A lot managed to get accomplished over the past couple of days at the spa." He took a bite of the filet mignon, which was scrumptious. "My dad really seems to love Mandy. In a very meaningful way."

"I think so too."

"I never thought I'd feel close to my dad," he said. "But I guess he really opened up and I saw him a new way. He said some things right before the ceremony that kinda got me choked up, actually."

"I'm really happy to hear that," she said. "We

had the right idea—to get married at the spa and bring them together. Our master plan worked."

"I think my feeling closer to my dad is why I brought up your mom earlier," he said. "But I don't want to interfere in that. That's for you to decide."

She reached across the table and squeezed his hand.

"I got you something," he said, standing up. "A little something. A wedding present."

Her face lit up. "Asher. You didn't have to do that."

"Well, when we were in town yesterday and you went into the bookstore and I took the twins to the coffee shop? There was a shop next door and I saw it in the window, so I stopped in…" He went over to his coat, reached into the pocket and handed her the little wrapped velvet box.

"What is it?" she asked.

He sat back down. "You have to open it and see."

She grinned and then ripped off the paper, opened the lid and gasped. "Oh, Asher." She held up the antique twenty-four-karat gold oval locket. It opened with space for a small photograph.

She'd always said she wanted a locket, an oval antique one, but that there was no point since she wouldn't know what kind of photo to put inside. She'd lost her father so young that she didn't remember him. A photo of her parents from the brief happy time they'd been together as a family would just break her heart, she'd once told him. And she'd never had a pet since she'd always worked long hours. *Maybe one day when I get married and have kids*, she'd said a couple of times.

That day was today.

"It's so beautiful," she said, staring at it. "Thank you."

"You can put a tiny photo of the twins in there," he said.

She smiled but her eyes were a little misty. "You remembered how much I always wanted one. But I never had the photograph to put inside. Now I do." She stood up. "Will you put it on me?"

"Sure," he said as she turned around and lifted up her hair, her delectable neck exposed in the floaty dress and so kissable. Her perfume was killing him. As was her creamy skin.

His hands brushed against the top of her back as he attached the clasp. Electric. "There you go."

She turned around. Still so close. "Thank you." She threw her arms around him and squeezed and he wrapped his own arms around her. Then she looked up, her eyes so sultry, her lips so irresistible, and he was suddenly kissing her.

And she was kissing him back.

"Asher," she whispered, her lips pressed up against his.

He deepened the kiss, one hand in her hair, the other on her neck, then around her waist, then both hands around her shoulders. "I can't stop kissing you."

"Don't stop," she whispered.

He took her hand and led her upstairs to her room since it was the first past the landing. *Don't think*, he ordered himself, barely able to anyway. *Just do.*

"I need a little help with the zipper." She turned around, her back to him, and he trailed kisses along her neck as she slid the zipper down. She turned back around and let the dress fall to the floor, then began unbuttoning his shirt, kissing his chest as she went.

He closed his eyes, knowing if he looked at her, practically naked except for a lacy strapless bra and underwear, he'd be too close to losing control. He felt his shirt being pulled off, his belt buckle undone and flung away, his pants unbuttoned. He shrugged out of them and walked her over to the bed, kissing her down and lying on top of her.

"You are so beautiful," he whispered, his hands in her hair.

"You too," she whispered back.

And as he was exploring inside the lacy bra with his hands and mouth, he felt his boxer briefs being tugged down. He kicked them away and then took off the bra, his tongue across her nipples making her arch and moan. He moved down her body slowly until he could use his teeth to pull down her tiny white lacy undies.

She let out another breathy moan that almost undid him, then reached into the bedside table for a condom.

"I'll do the honors," she said with a sultry smile.

After that he lost the ability to process thought. He could only feel every incredible sensation.

What felt like hours later, they lay beside each other, catching their breath. He could have sworn he heard her whisper "I love you," but when he looked over at her, she seemed to be fast asleep, her breath soft, her chest rising up and down, up and down.

He stared up at the ceiling, feeling like his tie was tightening around his neck, though he was buck naked. This was just going too fast. Too far, too fast.

He was grateful she was asleep. Because he couldn't have said anything back to her just then. He couldn't say anything without wrecking their wedding night. And that was the last thing he wanted.

And he couldn't keep hurting her either. Which was all he was doing with his inability to keep his hands off her and then feeling like the walls were closing in on him afterward. Closing in on their friendship.

What the morning would bring was another story. Part of the *take it as it comes* that made things hard instead of easy. Platonic would have kept things easy, kept a separation between them. He'd have known what the morning would bring. Coffee, barn chores, playing with the twins, breakfast. A trip into town.

Now she'd said "I love you" after they'd had sex. That added a whole new dimension.

And he wasn't ready for it. Didn't want to go there.

But trying to be platonic with Katie was just impossibly hard.

What the hell was he going to do?

A fussing baby woke Katie up at 2:13 a.m. Declan. She glanced over at the big bed—she was alone. But Declan was still fussing. Not full-out crying. She wasn't surprised the sounds had woken her; she'd always woken at the first peep coming from their bassinet. But if Asher wasn't in her bed and he wasn't in the nursery scooping up the crier...

Her heart plummeted.

He must have woken up earlier and gone back to his own bedroom.

She bit her lip and got out of bed, grabbing her terry bathrobe and tying it around her. Suddenly she felt exposed instead of like a woman who'd had incredible sex. The first time since giving birth. The first time since she'd conceived the twins.

She remembered thinking over and over *I love you, Ash,* as she was drifting off, but had she actually said it aloud? Maybe.

And maybe it had sent him over the edge. Great sex he could deal with, maybe. An *I love you* following it—probably not so much. She hurried into the nursery, trying to remember that building this new relationship with Asher would take time, and she'd have to go a few steps back to go one step forward. Patience, she reminded herself.

At least she'd had the wedding night of her dreams. She'd always have that memory. Always.

Of course, the fact that he'd left the bed they'd shared to be alone, to keep them separate, to put a gulf between them, hurt like hell. And she'd remember *that* too. She frowned, her chest aching.

In the nursery, she found Declan still fussy but his eyes were closed and he seemed to be soothing himself back to sleep. She let him be for a moment, but no, the little eyes opened and he let out a wail that probably woke the goats.

She heard footsteps coming and couldn't turn

toward the doorway. Couldn't bear to see the expression on his face. The *I'm sorry.* Maybe she could handle it in the cold light of day. But not right now. Not at two fifteen in the morning.

"I've got it," she said, her eyes on Declan as she rocked him.

"You sure?" he asked.

She nodded, still unable, unwilling to look at him.

She could feel him tensing in the doorway. *This is how it starts*, he was probably thinking. *And now you can't even look at me.*

Just go, she wanted to yell at him. But that would only make things worse.

Because she knew him so well, she could tell he was staring hard at her, then the ground, then back at her, trying to decide what to do, if he should say something. There was nothing he could say that would help things right now. They both knew that.

And then a moment later, he did go. Leaving her alone in the nursery.

She reached up to touch the locket he'd given her, then sat down in the rocker with Declan, needing that sweet weight in her arms, his little face to focus on. She could not be alone in her room, alone in the bed where she and Asher had just made love. On their wedding night.

This is not going to be easy, she said silently to

Declan, watching his lip quirk. *But I have faith in your daddy. Things are going to be okay.*

She said it and wanted to mean it. But right now, she wasn't all that sure.

Chapter Fourteen

At just past 7:00 a.m., as he spread fresh hay in the goats' pen, Asher got a text from a town Santa committee member asking if he could take on a Santa shift this morning at the hut on the town green. The scheduled Mr. Claus wrenched his back last night and they were expecting a big line of kids on a Sunday morning. Asher knew the guy, a cattle rancher ten miles up the road. He texted back You got it.

You're the best, Joanna Gomez texted back with three Santa hat emojis.

No, I'm the worst, he thought as he raked the hay, the twins in their stroller watching him with curious eyes. Out the window he could see the six goats pushing their noses in the coating of snow in the pasture, two jumping up on their favorite logs. He moved the stroller over to the window so the boys could see the goats having fun.

He sighed as he put away the rake. He'd messed up last night. And then things had gotten awkward, as he knew they would from the minute he'd felt the stirring toward Katie the first night she was back.

He heard the barn door opening and there was Katie in her blue down jacket and pink wool hat, with a mug of coffee in her hands.

"There everyone is!" she said brightly, taking a sip of her coffee. She went over to the twins in their stroller and leaned down to kiss each on their fleece-capped heads. She straightened and looked at him. "Let's not talk about it, okay?"

"Maybe we should," he said. "I don't want miscommunication or 'I thought this, you thought that' getting in our way, Katie."

She settled herself on the tall stool and took a sip of coffee. "Okay, here's what I think I know. We have clearly moved beyond friendship. There's nothing platonic about our relationship when we want to rip each other's clothes off and did just that last night. But, this makes you uneasy. You're worried a sexual and romantic relationship will blow up in our faces and end up breaking up our friendship and our family. You don't want to risk that so you're unwilling to commit to moving forward with the new us. You want to stick to the old us. Even though that's impossible."

That was it exactly. It was scary how perceptive she was. It meant he had to be honest because she would see through any crap. "Not impossible," he said. "Wouldn't you like to protect twenty-five years of friendship?"

She stared at him hard. "From what, though, Asher? From ourselves? From progress? From sex? From how we really feel about each other? I don't think putting up fake boundaries is going to help us."

He sighed. "I know."

"The reason you went back to your room last night," she said, slowly, "is about your unease and worry. So let's deal with that."

"How?" he asked.

"By doing what we've been doing. We keep going. We do what feels right while respecting each other's feelings. Leaving felt right to you last night. I need to be okay with that and give you the space and time to work through your discomfort with how things are progressing between us. And you need to understand that what you do affects me and how I feel."

"Understanding and maybe a little compromising," he said.

"A good start. I can work with that."

"What would you rather I'd done last night?" he asked. "Instead of just leaving your bed in the middle of the night?"

"Woken me up and said, 'Katie, I'm feeling uneasy, same old stuff, and I need to go back to my room for some space. But the sex was *amazing* and you are a goddess.'" She grinned and relief flooded him.

"It *was* amazing," he agreed. *And yes, you are a goddess.*

"Yeah, it was," she said, shooting him a smile that went straight to his heart.

"I agreed to take a Santa shift at ten. Three hours. That's a lot of kids." He did the math. Five minutes per kid times four times three.

"Aww, that's sweet that you're doing that. Gigi texted a little while ago and asked if I was free for lunch and Christmas shopping with the twins, so that's great timing. We can meet up after."

"Sounds good," he said. "I'll miss you and the boys."

She looked at him for a moment. "Me too. It'll be the first time we've been apart since Friday. We like having you around, Asher Dawson."

He walked over to her and took her mug and put it on the other stool nearby, then wrapped his arms around her and hugged her tight.

He was so grateful that she did. And that she seemed to really understand him. Because they needed each other. The four of them. And nothing could ruin that.

Especially not *him*.

"Mr. Santa," five-year-old Thomas with the red hair and freckles said, "I know what I want for Christmas."

Asher smiled at the "Mr. Santa." That was a first. He was on hour two in the Santa hut in head-to-toe costume, and his head was spinning with the gift lists and explanations of how good the kids had been that year. The big bushy beard was a little itchy, but it was cold outside and the thick red-and-white suit and black boots were keeping him warm. Outside was a long line of kids waiting with their parents, Christmas songs piped in from somewhere. There were craft tables alongside the hut on both sides with make-your-own ornaments and paper and markers, so kids could sit and do something fun until their number was called.

"I want a big yellow truck that dumps stuff," the boy went on. "And a scooter and a new helmet with spikes. And French fries every night with dinner. No vegetables. And new cars and a track to race them."

"You must have been really good this year to want all that," Asher said.

Thomas nodded, his red bangs flopping. "I've been mostly good."

The volunteer on elf duty, whose job it was to let the youngster know his time with Santa was up, popped her head in. "Okay, honey, grab a candy cane on your way out."

The boy happily ran out, and a little girl came in, maybe eight years old. She had freckles, like Katie, and wore a bright pink hat with a pom-pom.

"Ho, ho, ho, and merry Christmas!" Asher said from his seat on the big red-and-white-striped "throne."

"What's your name, dear?"

"Lucy and I'm eight. Santa, can you make wishes come true? I don't mean a present, but like a wish?"

"I can try my best," Asher said.

"My mom and dad are getting a divorce," she said, her brown eyes getting misty. "And I don't want them to. Can you make it stop?"

Asher felt a stab in the direction of his heart. "I don't think I have that kind of magical power," he said. "But I know how it feels. My parents got divorced when I was about your age."

"Really?" she asked, eyes widening. "Was it horrible? Did you have two houses?"

"Well, I did have two houses. Three if you count my grandparents' ranch. I spent a lot of time there. I liked school and I had friends so I was okay."

"I like school and I have a best friend named Elodie and another named Jamie. We have a best friend club."

Asher smiled. "Good. I'm still best friends with my bestie from kindergarten."

"Is that like fifty years?" she asked.

"Not quite," he said with a smile.

"What's his name?"

"*Her* name. Katie."

"Are you gonna marry her?" Lucy asked, head tilted. "Because who else would you marry besides your best friend?"

Put that way, he had to agree.

"Actually I did," he said. *Just yesterday, in fact. And I'm already making a mess of the best thing that ever happened to me: Katie Crosby.*

"Mrs. Claus is named Katie? I didn't know that."

Asher grinned. "Yep. She's the best." He held up his left hand, his gold wedding band shining in the dim little hut with its faux plastic window.

"Of course she is," the girl said. "She's Mrs. Claus!"

True again.

"And I go to my nana Jane's house a lot," Lucy added. "She's teaching me how to bake Christmas cookies. She's so nice."

"My gram was really nice too," he said, picturing Cassie Dawson tending to her goats, putting stickers on her jars of milk and cheese, letting him do a batch of stickers when he got good at centering them.

"I don't want my parents to get a divorce," Lucy said, her eyes filling with tears. She stared down at her pink sneakers.

"I know. I didn't want my parents to either. But you know what helped me?"

She looked up. "What?"

"My grandmother gave me some good ideas to help me through it. She told me that when I was upset, I should say so. If I was feeling sad or scared or just needed a hug, I should let my mom or my dad or both of them know. I shouldn't keep my thoughts and feelings to myself. Even if they were mean or scary thoughts."

"Did your parents get mad at you?" she asked.

"Nope," he said. "Sometimes they didn't realize that I was feeling so bad. So telling them helped them and me. And I talked to my grandmother a lot about how I was feeling. I could tell her anything."

"I can tell my nana anything too. She likes to hear my thoughts on things."

He smiled. "That makes you really lucky. We only have around five minutes left. Do you want to tell me what you want for Christmas?"

"What I really want is a new bike. A red one with a silver water bottle holder and a bell."

"Well, I wish you a very merry Christmas, Lucy."

"You too, Santa!" she said. "Say hi to Katie Claus!" she added before running out just as the elf popped her head in.

Katie Claus. He just might think of her that way forever.

A few more kids later and Asher needed a really large, really strong cup of coffee. During his break, when he got a small foam cup of weak town hall coffee, which would have to do until the end of his shift, he texted Katie to see how she was. She texted back immediately, telling him she'd met Gigi in town and they were shopping, then would have lunch at the brick oven pizzeria and then do more shopping. She might need a foot massage later, she'd added.

The three dots indicating she was still typing went on for a good thirty seconds, then disappeared. She was worried about the foot massage request, he realized. Because of what happened last night. He texted back.

You remember my foot massages are legendary. Shop away. I've got you.

She texted back a happy face wearing a Santa

hat, then wrote that she'd meet him at the Christmas tree at 2:00 p.m. so she could pick a gift wish, and they'd stop at the animal shelter and see the dogs. If you think we're in a good enough place to adopt that Australian shepherd we always talked about.

His heart wrenched. Then he wrote back.

We're going to be fine.

They had to be. End of story.

He got back a smiley face, but he could feel her worry by just looking at the yellow emoji.

He texted back a note that he'd meet her at two and added a Santa hat emoji because Katie was a big user of emojis. This time he got back a smiley face with a cowboy hat on it and six goats and two babies in Santa hats.

That he couldn't wait to see her wasn't lost on him. He missed the twins fiercely, especially after being surrounded by children for the past hour and a half. But he needed to see his Katie just as desperately.

After a delicious lunch at the brick oven pizzeria, where the twins had thankfully napped in their stroller the entire time so that Katie and Gigi could *really* talk, they headed out onto Main Street, ready to hit the shops again. Katie had told her friend everything—about the two days at the spa, the wedding and then last night and this morning.

"My wedding present sure did its job," Gigi said with a grin.

"Dinner was such a surprise and so romantic." Katie sighed. "Thank you so much, Gigi. I don't know what I'd do without you."

"You can make it up to me later when I text you a thousand photos of table centerpieces. You can help me choose. My mother likes the ones I think are eh."

Katie smiled. "You got it. So you really think I'm gonna get my Christmas wish?" she asked as they walked down the street slowly, Katie maneuvering the big stroller around people and dogs coming their way. It was twelve thirty and Bear Ridge was bustling with holiday shoppers.

Gigi was a great listener and very thoughtful about giving advice, and had insisted that she and Asher would be the couple Katie hoped for by Christmas. "I really do. Asher is feeling his way through this. Like I said, he had a plan and it fell to pot, like a lot of plans do. He's trying to control something that can't be controlled." Gigi wiggled her eyebrows.

Katie laughed. And Gigi was once again exactly right. That was precisely what Asher was doing—it was about controlling the uncontrollable. Their feelings for each other.

"Sounds like seeing his dad's love life issues played out in front of him helped too," Gigi said as she stopped to peer at the Christmas display in the used bookstore window. "He's been cynical about marriage and things working out his whole life. You're his safe zone. Then he actually lost you for an entire year. Now not only does he have you back, but he has baby twins. He must be feeling incredibly protective, not just of you and the boys, but of himself. I get it."

"I do too," Katie said as they moved on, stopping at the next window, which was the town's general store and gift shop and had all sorts of interesting things for sale. "It's just hard to go through the journey when what I want is the destination."

Gigi nodded and pulled open the door, Katie waiting for a small group of shoppers to exit before pushing in the big stroller. "I know what you mean. But the journey with all its annoying curves and detours will get you there."

Katie nodded, really thinking about that. It was true. "I'd like to find a wedding present for Asher. And a thank-you gift for his dad and Mandy. And something for Axel and Sadie, who ranch-sat for us while we were gone."

"This is definitely the place. Ooh, I'm gonna

go check out the intimates section for myself," Gigi said and dashed over to the area at the back of the store. Katie eyed the silk robes and fleece-lined pj's. Asher would probably like fleece-lined pj's.

A very sexy black satin teddy with a low cut lacy V-neck called to Katie for herself. But she should definitely *not* push things. And things didn't seem to need to be pushed anyway, she thought with a smile.

She walked around the shop, glad it wasn't too crowded since the stroller took up lots of room. She bought two cute stuffed rattles for the twins, a beautiful pair of beeswax candles and two rose quartz holders with a special tag about their restorative powers for Mandy and John, since she knew those would haves special meaning. For Axel and Sadie she bought a big festive tin of different kinds of popcorn, since she recalled Asher mentioning that they loved caramel popcorn. And now she just had to find a wedding gift for Asher. Something meaningful. Truly special. She'd thought about making him a photo book with pictures from over the years and now, with the twins. She'd probably do that for Christmas. But she wanted to get him something special as a wedding gift, as special as the locket he'd given her.

The minute she saw the Christmas sweater on

a stack on a table, she knew she'd found it. It was the traditional goofy ugly Christmas sweater, so colorful and tacky she could barely look at it without her eyes hurting. There was an earnest Santa and a cartoon reindeer and dancing snow globes with elf faces around the border. And in the center in big red and green letters was "North Pole Daddy." The sweater would make him laugh and she had to get it. It spoke to their tradition of who could find the ugliest of ugly Christmas sweaters.

Just when she and Gigi had made it to the door with the many packages on their wrists and in the baskets under the twins' stroller, Katie froze. Her mother was coming into the shop.

"Oh, hello!" Celia Crosby said. Once again, she looked great, her honey-colored straight hair just above her shoulders, shiny and clean. She had a little makeup on and wore a cranberry-colored wool peacoat and jeans with leather boots.

Katie moved back to let her mother inside. "Gigi, have you ever met my mother, Celia Crosby?" She turned to Celia. "This is my friend Gigi Robertson. She's an officer with the Bear Ridge PD. We were rookies together."

"Actually, your mother came to see me soon after the news of your death," Gigi said. "We had a lovely conversation. I think it helped both of us.

Celia came to see me a few times at the PD over the past year."

Katie glanced from Gigi to her mother. She remembered Celia mentioning she'd gone to the police station after the social worker began helping her. Before Katie had faked her death, Gigi hadn't known her mother or much about her other than that she'd had a troubled life and Katie had had to grow up in foster care because of it. If Katie had been on the force a couple years earlier, she probably would have arrested her mother for something or other. A few times.

"I'd better get going," Gigi said. "Nice to see you, Celia. You're looking very well." She turned to Katie and handed her a large box. "This is for you and Asher. Another wedding present." She grinned, gave each baby a caress on their fleece-capped heads, then left.

"A wedding present?" Celia repeated. Her gaze went straight to Katie's left hand, where the silver wedding band had joined the engagement ring.

"We got married yesterday, actually," Katie said.

"Oh, well, isn't that wonderful. Congratulations."

This was so awkward. Katie wanted to run out of the shop *and* stay and talk. Her mother would always have a powerful grip on her heart. Celia always had.

"I didn't know you went to see Gigi," Katie said.

"I was so shocked at the reports about your death. I knew you worked at the PD, so I went there for more information, anything, really, more than what I heard on the news."

Katie remembered thinking about her mother as she'd dragged herself from the water last December, how Celia Crosby wouldn't even know she'd "died," wouldn't care much because she'd be too strung out for the news to even penetrate. If she'd heard the news at all. It was hard enough knowing what the news would do to Asher, but that Katie didn't have a family who'd mourn was one of the reasons she'd been able to go through with the plan.

"I spoke to a really nice officer named Ford Dawson," Celia continued, "who said he'd been your training partner. And then he directed me to Gigi. He told me the two of you were close friends. Gigi and I had lunch that day in the break room. I looked pretty bad then, was still using, but she wasn't judgmental about that. She let me sit with her and then we ordered in lunch and just sat and cried together."

Katie bit her lip, wanting to hear more, yet

wanting her mother to stop talking. Why was this so confusing?

"I told her a bit of my story," Celia continued, "and that I was living in a shelter and that a social worker was mentoring me, but I was still so broken up about you. Gigi gave me some good advice and information about getting clean and the name of a good rehab in Brewster. She said she'd drive me over if I didn't have a way of getting there, which I didn't. How kind she was. The next day I told her I wanted to go and wouldn't let you down, Katie."

"I didn't know that," she said—for the second time, her heart dipping. "Any of that." Perhaps Gigi hadn't brought it up the two times they'd seen each other since Katie's return because she'd figured it was Katie and her mother's business.

"I was in bad shape when I went to see her that first time. But after about six months, I'd gotten myself together. And I had a job and an apartment. Gigi told me you'd be proud of me. That meant a lot to me. That she thought so."

Katie felt her eyes sting with tears. "I am proud of you for that."

"Do you think we could get together?" Celia asked shyly. "Have dinner? Either at my apartment or your house?"

Katie froze. She could see the hope on Celia's

face. But all she could remember right now was the hope in her own heart over the years. Constantly stomped on. How did she just suddenly trust this woman who was like a stranger, really?

Celia's expression said she was bracing for a no. Katie's chest felt tight, but she could get through a dinner, a first start—if Asher were there. "Why don't you come for dinner tomorrow night. At Dawson's Sweet Dairy Ranch. It's about eight miles out from here."

Celia's eyes lit up. "I've driven out there a couple times over the past year. I remembered it's where a social worker once told me you spent a lot of time with Asher. So I wanted to see it."

"How about six thirty?" Katie asked. "That way the twins will be awake a bit while you're there."

This time her mother's entire face lit up. She looked from Katie to the twins, then back at Katie. "That would be great. I'm really excited about this, Katie. Thank you."

Katie managed a smile, but her stomach was churning. "See you tomorrow."

Thank heavens she was meeting Asher in a little while. Because she really needed her best friend right now.

Chapter Fifteen

"I'll make dinner so you two can have some privacy," Asher said after Katie told him about running into her mom. "But I'll be right there in the kitchen and I'll be there at the dining table." He could tell just from her voice and the set of her shoulders how anxious she was about this, how it was weighing on her.

Katie wrapped her arm around his and pulled closer to him. "Good. Thank you. I can do this if you're there."

They were walking toward the beautiful lit up Christmas tree on the town green. "Let's go pick a few wish requests from the tree," he said. "I plucked one the day I thought I saw you here, pushing the stroller."

"Wait, you never told me you thought you saw me and the twins."

"Huh, I guess I didn't. When you revealed yourself at the ranch, I was in total shock and then we were just full speed ahead on all the new stuff."

"How did you recognize me?" she asked.

"I'd know you anywhere, Katie Crosby. Yeah, you had long blond hair, big black sunglasses, a hat pulled down low and all, but I know your walk and the way you hold yourself."

She smiled. "That's Katie Crosby *Dawson*. Or it will be when I fill out the forms at the town hall tomorrow. These guys will be Dawsons too."

He kneeled down in front of the stroller, the twins' curious blue eyes on him. It seemed Dylan could go a solid minute without blinking. "Team Dawson," he said, kissing each boy on their hatted heads.

Katie grinned. "I love that. It makes me really feel part of a family."

"Well, you are, even without the name," he said. "Same for them."

She closed her eyes and reached out her hand and picked a little plastic pouch. She unhooked it and slid out the paper. "'My Christmas wish is a fluffy dog bed for my dog Jasper. His old one is almost totally flat. Thank you. From BK. Age nine. Bear Ridge.' Awww," Katie said. "I'm getting the fluffiest dog bed I can find for Jasper."

Asher smiled and took off a wish request. He planned to fulfill at least three. "'I don't believe in dumb wishes because nothing ever comes true anyway,'" he read. "'But if they do, I really want a pair of Air Jordan sneakers size five. And my mom wants snow boots cuz her old ones are leaking. Size eight. Can you make the boots from me? If I had any money I'd buy them for her but I don't. From Jaden, eight years old.'" Asher let out a breath. "I can just see this kid. Cynical like me at his age. Not believing in much. But here he is, caring about his mother's leaky snow boots. Yeah, he's getting his Air Jordans. Next size up too. And I'll probably throw in a basketball."

"You have a big heart, Asher," Katie said.

"Thanks." He reached for the stroller. "Now let's go to the animal shelter and see if there are any Australian shepherds."

Katie grinned. "I'm so excited about the possibilities."

"Me too," he said.

Asher picked one more wish request and tucked it in his pocket to read and take care of later. Then they packed the twins and their stroller in the trunk and headed for the Bear Ridge Animal Shelter.

But ten minutes later, they were both disappointed. Not only weren't there any Australian shepherds or mixes, there were no dogs at all. A wonderful thing for the shelter, since an adoption event over the weekend had been a huge success. The shelter director offered to take their name and number and promised to call if anything even resembling an Australian shepherd came in.

"I just realized we completely forgot about getting a tree," Katie said as they turned onto the quarter-mile drive to the ranch.

"Let's go get one now. We can do it fast before Declan or Dylan lets out a single shriek. I can run in and pick out one I know you'll like."

"I have total trust in you on that." He knew what her dream Christmas tree was. The trees at the group foster homes she'd live in had both been artificial with no lights allowed due to fire hazard, so they'd just had garland and ornaments. Once she'd moved out, he'd always surprised her with a ridiculously big real tree with a ton of multicolored lights. This year, he'd outdo himself.

Fifteen minutes later, Asher had a seven-foot Fraser fir on the top of his truck. As he hopped back in the warm pickup, he said, "I know what we're doing tonight."

She grinned. "I'm really excited about decorating it. It's the twins' first Christmas. And ours as a family. I feel really lucky. Australian shepherd collie or no Australian shepherd."

"Me too," he said, his gaze dropping to her pink-red lips. He forced his eyes up and onto the road. He couldn't wait to get home.

The tree was in a stand by the sliding glass doors and completely naked. It was so majestic, so beautiful, and smelled so good that for a second, Katie could see just leaving it like that. But nah. The fun was just beginning.

She hurried over to where the twins were in their bouncers, Christmas music playing softly, and tilted them so they had a better view of the tree. "Your first Christmas is going to be so special."

"Yeah, it is," Asher said, coming down the stairs from the attic. "Got the box of ornaments. And your box labeled Christmas."

She bit her lip. "I can't believe you went to the trouble of taking all my ornaments off the tree in my apartment last year and saving them. Well, I can believe it. Of course you did that. Thanks to you, I have all my favorite clothes and my warm down jacket."

"One of my cousins asked if I was going to donate your things," he said, setting down the boxes on the coffee table. "But I couldn't see doing that right away. Or as the year went on. Honestly, I think forty years from now, if you hadn't come back, your stuff would still be in whatever attic I had. Which reminds me. If you hadn't come back, I'd be carting all those boxes and duffel bags to a new place right about now. I wouldn't be able to stay here much longer."

"Where would you have gone?" she asked. "Would you have bought a ranch in Bear Ridge?"

"I'm really not sure. I was really pissed off when I realized I couldn't take my grandmother's goats with me—they were ranch property. So the idea of starting another ranch in Cassie's honor didn't feel right without them."

"I can see that," she said, coming over and opening her Christmas box. "Asher, look at this. Right on top." She held up an ornament she'd made in elementary school, a paper heart with a small photograph of her and Asher in third grade. "That's gotta go on the tree. It's tradition that it goes on first." She didn't have a lot of her old things, especially because there was no parent saving her elementary school artwork, but some things she'd managed to keep hold of, even through the two group homes.

"I took that ornament off last," he said. "That's why it's on top. It was two days after Christmas last year when I found out you left everything you had to me. So I went to your apartment and the first thing I saw was the tree and this ornament front and center. I bawled, Katie. I had to leave and come back the next day."

"Aww," she said, touching his arm. "I'm so sorry, Asher." She could imagine how heartbroken he'd been. Not only to lose his best friend, but because of their argument, those final words, the way she'd driven off in the snow.

"Well," he said, his voice heavy with emotion. "You're here and that's all that matters."

A half hour later, the lights were twirled, the ornaments were hung, a star was at the top and Asher did the honors of turning on the switch. The tree lit up so beautifully that Katie's eyes got misty. And once again, she went right into his arms for a hug.

This time, though, he didn't kiss her.

They did have an audience. The twins were staring at them.

Katie laughed. "I love that they're so curious. Look at those big eyes." She glanced at the big silver wrapped box on the coffee table. "I almost want to put that gift under the tree, but it's actually a wedding present from Gigi and her fiancé."

"Let's open it," he said.

They sat down on the sofa, the twins' eyes still on them. Katie ripped off the paper and lifted the lid.

Asher pulled out four sets of matching red-and-green-plaid flannel pajamas Hers, his and two sets in size three-to-six months. Katie held up the baby pj's. "Adorable."

"I say we make dinner and then afterward, get changed into our 'wedding meets Christmas' pj's and take goofy selfies," Asher said. "Who knew I'd have a family Christmas card to send out?"

Katie grinned. "Love it."

Could she be happier right now? No. Things might not be exactly perfect between them, but right now, life was as good as it got. Katie tossed all the pj's into the washer using the twins' scent-less detergent and got that going, then they went into the kitchen, opening up the fridge and cabinets until they decided on chicken parm and spaghetti and garlic bread.

For the next twenty minutes, they cooked together, chatting with the boys in their high chairs, each taking a break from their spot at the stove or counter to give a baby a bottle. Just before they sat down to eat, Katie put the wash in the dryer.

After dinner—and ice cream for dessert—they went upstairs, each holding a baby. They started in the nursery, getting the boys into their new pj's, then, leaving them in their playpen, Katie and Asher headed into their rooms to change.

They met in the hallway and laughed at how matchy-matchy they were, then each grabbed a baby and went back downstairs.

"How about we get a shot with us in front of

the tree?" Katie asked. "Can you prop up one of our phones and set the timer to take the pic after ten seconds?"

Katie got settled on the rug in front of the tree, a baby in each of her arms while Asher fussed with the phone, which fell over a couple of times. Finally, he got it set up and dashed over and sat down beside her. Asher moved Declan onto his lap, and Katie settled Dylan on hers.

"Say cheeseburgers!" Asher said.

Katie had no idea if the babies were smiling or ready to screech with exhaustion. But when Asher got up to check the photo, it was so funny and perfect that Katie wouldn't change a thing. Mommy and Daddy had big smiles, but each baby couldn't have looked more bored.

"It's a keeper," Katie said.

The doorbell rang and they both shrugged at who it could possibly be, Asher walking over to open it.

It was John Dawson. Looking flustered.

"Uh-oh," Asher said, holding the door open wide.

"I think maybe you two were like our own special healing crystal when you were with us," John said. He looked them up and down. "Maybe I should get us a pair of those matching pajamas." He twisted his lips and looked completely dejected.

"Come on in, Dad," Asher said. "I'll make some coffee. We have tiramisu and ice cream."

"Just coffee. I don't think I could eat a bite."

"You two talk," Katie said. "I'll put the twins to bed." She brought them into the kitchen so that Daddy and Grandpa could kiss them good-night, then headed upstairs. The twins were so tired that they conked out fast and easily transferred into their bassinets.

When she came back downstairs, Asher and his father had moved into the living room with their mugs of coffee. She poured herself one and joined them.

"Is it so wrong to want to take a week's vacation to Vegas with the guys?" he asked. "Boy, did Mandy get upset."

"Well, you two are still newlyweds," Katie said. "You've been married only thirteen months. Maybe she doesn't like the idea of you wanting to spend a week away so soon?"

"That's what she said. That we're newlyweds. And I'd be away for Valentine's Day, which apparently is a very busy time at the spa. The whole week."

"Valentine's Day is special," Katie said.

John took a sip of his coffee. "I'd get her a really great gift."

"I think it's more that she wants you to want to

be with her, Dad. Valentine's is a special holiday for couples. Especially for newlyweds."

"You two already made big plans?" John asked.

Katie swallowed. Asher would get her a gag gift like he did every year, like ridiculous fuzzy socks with pink hearts all over them, and a big box of chocolates, also like he did every year. She would not expect anything more.

"We're still planning the honeymoon," Asher said. He turned to Katie. "I got a text not five minutes ago from my cousin Noah. The Dawsons are offering a cabin for a few days and use of the entire dude ranch, including the day care, as a wedding gift. Maybe we can go for New Year's."

"Ooh," Katie said. "That sounds heavenly. We can go riding and hiking and fish and hang out in the lodge. It's so beautifully decorated for Christmas."

"Sounds really good to me too," Asher said.

John sighed and took a long sip of his coffee. "I wish Mandy and I were on the same page like you two are."

"Dad, I'm gonna give you the same advice I gave you at the spa. And that's to put Mandy first. Even when it doesn't come naturally. When you do that, there will come a point when Mandy won't think twice about you going away with your buddies for a week, because it's a special event and she'll want to make you happy too. But when you put yourself first as a given, it's going to create tension and make her feel like she's not special."

"Is that so, Katie?" John asked, looking at her with hopeful eyes that she'd tell him Asher had it wrong.

"It's so," Katie confirmed. "Look, you were single a long time before you met Mandy. You got a little set in your ways. Just remember what really matters, John. Your *marriage*. You love Mandy. You want this marriage to last forever. So make that happen with what you do and say and think. Maybe before you make any decisions, stop and ask yourself: Will this help me accomplish my goals of having a happy marriage? If not, toss it from your mind."

"Huh," John said. "No wonder you two are running around in matching pj's. You really have this marriage thing down and it's been what? One day?"

Katie stole a glance at her husband. If only John knew what was really going on. She and Asher didn't have anything figured out. They were taking baby steps toward this new version of their friendship: a real relationship.

John bolted up. "I get it. I really get it. I'm gonna text Mandy that I took a long drive to think things over and that I'm on my way home."

"That's a good idea, Dad," Asher said, standing up too.

They walked John to the door and he hurried out into the cold. They both held up hands to wave, watching as the red taillights disappeared down the drive.

"I was an idiot to think it would be that easy for them to work things out," Asher said as he shut the door. "They'll be divorced by Valentine's Day at this rate."

"Nah," Katie said, her stomach churning. "Don't say that. Your dad is just figuring things out as he goes. Kind of like we are."

Asher sighed. "Well, failure is not an option with us, Katie."

"I don't think it's an option for your dad either. Yeah, it's gonna be a little rough on him to figure out how to put his marriage first. But he'll get there. And he'll get the prize for doing so. The woman he loves and wants to grow old with."

But Katie could see Asher wasn't so sure about that. His expression told her all the good will he'd stored up about the possibility of a marriage working out in his family had blown to bits.

Relationships, marriages don't work out, Asher had been saying his entire life. Katie had listened to his diatribes on the subject for years. *You know what lasts?* he'd say. *Friendship. Real friendship. I don't know what I'd do without you...*

So take your own advice, Asher Dawson. Put the marriage first. Don't find out again what you'd do without me!

She knew that tonight, at least, they would not be sharing a bed in their matching flannel pj's. But his dad throwing a monkey wrench into things could be helpful. Because it would force Asher to deal with all these issues that had been plaguing him since childhood. About marriage and romance and lasting love. He'd have to keep his own eye on the prize. His own marriage.

Katie sighed. She'd give him tonight and not push. But what she would give to have her husband beside her in bed. Their bed.

Chapter Sixteen

"The tree is beautiful," Celia Crosby said the next evening as she stepped into the living room.

Katie smiled. Her mother had been exactly on time at six thirty. Celia wore a long red cable-knit sweater and red-and-green-plaid pants that reminded Katie so much of the new family pj's that the sight of them kept poking at her heart.

Katie had spent few Christmases with her mother. During supervised visitation at the group homes, her mother had not shown up to two scheduled Christmas Day visits. She'd shown up other years, high out of her mind and ranting. Five years ago, Celia had come to Katie's apartment building, screaming up at the window for money, saying, "Where is your Christmas spirit for your mama?"

You told Asher you wouldn't rehash, Katie reminded herself as Celia stepped deeper into the room, her gaze on the twins in their bouncers on the rug near the sofa. She certainly didn't mean to. The memories were just *right there*.

"Here you go," Asher said to her mother as he came out of the kitchen carrying a glass of cranberry juice.

"Thank you, Asher," Celia said, taking a sip and then setting it down on a coaster on the coffee table. She looked at each of them. "Could I hold the twins? Just for a moment."

Katie hesitated and glanced at Asher, who didn't rush to respond; he was letting her decide what she was comfortable with. "Why don't you have a seat on the sofa or that really comfortable chair, and I'll bring Declan over to start."

Once again, Celia's face lit up. She sat down on the sofa, and Katie brought over her precious baby son. It wasn't easy to hand him over to her mother.

She won't drop him. Even if she does, he'll land on her lap or the sofa and I'll swoop right in and he'll be fine. Her mother seemed absolutely sober. Given that Katie had never seen her look this way before the past week, the difference was so startling that Katie didn't doubt her mother was not using drugs.

Celia held Declan carefully, looking down at him with an expression of wonder. "He's so beautiful. I didn't even know when I fought to change my life to honor yours that I would also have grandchildren. This is such a miracle."

Okay, time to ask the questions she'd always wanted answers to. Her mother had never been capable of giving her straight responses before. "I'd like to ask you something very personal," Katie said, staring at Celia.

"Anything," Celia said, looking up at her.

"Why did it take my supposed death to change your life? Why didn't you fight for me when I was alive? When I was a kid and needed you? Why only when I was gone?"

Celia took a breath. "That's a fair question. I think it was the shock. You were always so full of life and healthy and any time I saw you, you seemed just fine, even though I know now how hard things must have been. You lost your father and then you had to live with strangers in a group home. I'm so sorry, Katie. For everything."

Katie took that all in, but she didn't know what to say, how to respond; she barely knew how she felt.

Asher covered her hand with his for a moment before he stood up. He walked over to Celia. "Trade you Dylan for Declan?"

"Oh, I'd love to hold Dylan now," Celia said. She held out Declan, and Asher took him, then handed him to Katie, who clung on to him.

Asher brought Dylan over to Celia, who held him just as carefully and reverently as she had his twin.

Celia smiled. "You're precious like your brother." She gently caressed his soft brown hair. Dylan stared up at her with his big curious blue eyes. "For a while, when you were an infant, Katie, I was doing okay. I wasn't using. But then I got so nervous about being a bad mother that I turned into one. It's hard to even think of myself just abandoning you when you were so small. I'm so sorry, Katie." Tears streamed down Celia's cheeks.

Asher stood up and took Dylan so that Celia could have her hands free, and she immediately wiped her eyes.

"I appreciate hearing all this," Katie said. She wished she could give her mother more than that, but she couldn't. Maybe with time.

"I understand what you mean about being shocked when Katie reappeared," Asher said suddenly, looking at Celia. "It's how I felt." But he actually looked conflicted, as if he were thinking about something that wasn't adding up for him.

"Everything I'd said or done wrong where Katie was concerned, I wanted to undo."

Katie glanced at him. He caught her eye for a moment, then looked down at Declan. She wondered what he was thinking about in particular.

Declan let out a fussy wail and Dylan started squirming. Asher took Declan from Katie. "I'll get these guys to bed."

"I'd love to make dinner, if that's okay," Celia said. "I've gotten really good in the kitchen. Or we can cook together..." she prompted Katie.

"I was planning on steaks and baked potatoes," Katie said. "Sound good? I have a recipe for a great mushroom sauce from the woman who used to watch the twins while I worked."

"Sounds great," Celia said, standing up.

They headed into the kitchen, the big country room suddenly seeming smaller. Katie showed her mother where the potatoes were, and they got to work, Celia scrubbing the potatoes over the sink, Katie getting out the carton of mushrooms.

"This means so much to me," Celia said, turning to look at Katie. "I know it may take you a while to trust me."

All Katie could manage was a nod. She sucked in a breath, wishing this wasn't so overwhelming on every level. She also wished Asher was down here. Just so she could feel his presence, feel his support. He was probably giving her and her mother time to talk and be together one-on-one, but no matter how much Celia said and did the "right" things, Katie felt the walls closing in on her. Zero to sixty was just too fast.

This must be how Asher feels about going from best buds to a bed, she thought, mentally shaking her head.

"I'm surprised you and Asher haven't been married since age eighteen," Celia said, sliding the potatoes into the oven. "Any time I'd see you in town, you were always with him. Such a tall, handsome guy. You know, your dad and I were eighteen when we eloped."

Katie didn't know much about her parents' history. She barely remembered her father at all, just that she had warm and fuzzy feelings for him, that he'd been a good father.

"I didn't know that," Katie said, pausing from quartering the mushrooms. "You were high school sweethearts?"

"Not really. We'd just met at our summer job at a fast-food place that closed a long time ago. I was wild back then and he wasn't, but he fell for me. For a while there, I wanted to be the person he wished I was without all the drinking and drug use, but my addictions got the better of me."

"But he married you anyway?" she asked.

"He thought he could fix me. But that's the awful thing about addiction. It stomps on everyone you love. I used to always tell him we should have a baby, that that's the one thing I'd bet would get me clean for good, but he said he couldn't bring a baby into that kind of uncertainty, that it wasn't fair. But I did get pregnant when I was twenty and I was so happy. We were both so happy. I got clean and stayed clean till just a few weeks after you were born."

Katie's chest constricted. She loved the idea of the three of them being a happy family even for that brief time. "I'm glad you told me that. That makes me feel good. And happy for Dad. He must have been so relieved."

Celia seasoned the two steaks with salt and pepper and slid them into the cast-iron pan. "He was. But then I got scared of being a bad mother and fell back into old patterns and that was that. Your father told me to leave or go back to rehab and I thought I'd never beat it so I just left. I thought you were better off without me. Both of you. I know it sounds like an excuse, but I really believed that." She shook her head. "I think that's what kept me in such a sorry state for so long. Until I heard you were gone."

"You haven't used drugs since? Not once?" Katie asked.

"Not once," Celia said. "I made use of my sponsors, calling anytime I needed help. And I spent a lot of time looking at the one photograph I had of you. When you were a baby." She wiped her hands on a towel and reached into her pocket and pulled out a small photograph. She held it up. "You were four months old."

Katie peered at it. "Just a month older than the twins are now."

"I know I can't make up for anything, Katie. But I'd like a fresh start if you'll have me."

"I need time. But I'm glad you opened up."

Celia gave her a shaky smile, and Katie was standing so close to her mother that she could turn and open her arms and hug her. But she couldn't.

"Will you excuse me for a minute?" Katie said. "I'll be right back."

Celia nodded and Katie ran up the stairs into the nursery. Asher was there, sitting in the rocker with Dylan, who was sleeping, Declan also asleep in his bassinet.

She burst into tears and covered her face with her hands. "She told me everything and I understand and I want a relationship with her but I just can't. I can't bear it."

Asher stood and put Dylan in his bassinet, then rushed over to Katie and wrapped his arms around her. "I know it's hard. You're doing fine, Katie. One step at a time, right? You can't go from nothing to everything just like that. But if you want to have a relationship with your mother, you will. Trust, letting go, a new beginning—all that is going to take time."

Katie sucked in a breath, Asher's arms around her just the comfort she needed. She nodded against his navy Henley shirt. "I feel better. Thank you." She almost said, *I love you so much,* but she kept it to herself.

Katie went into the bathroom and splashed cold water on her face, then met Asher in the hallway and they headed downstairs for dinner, which smelled heavenly. She wrapped her arm around his and leaned her head against him, and he touched her face and smiled so empathetically at her that she let out a little sigh.

With Asher at her side, she could do anything.

Over the next week, Asher felt like he and Katie were falling into a good rhythm at the ranch. Each day they took turns waking up at the crack of dawn to take care of the goats and let them out of their pen while the other didn't have to put on four layers to stay warm and took care of the twins and fed them breakfast. Then they'd deliver the Dawson's Sweet Dairy Ranch milk to their clients in town and in Brewster, go out to lunch, do some Christmas shopping, particularly for the wish request recipients. Asher had gotten everything on his list for his wish requests and Katie was still looking for just the right matching ugly Christmas sweaters for a young married couple who'd both lost their jobs recently and had been invited to an ugly Christmas sweater party on Christmas Eve but had nothing to wear. He loved the sweater Katie had given him as a wedding gift and was saving it for Christmas Eve.

Katie had seen her mother twice since dinner last week. They'd met for coffee with the twins and the next time they'd all gone to the petting zoo at his cousin's dude ranch, which had moved indoors into the heated barn. Katie had said being out in public, having lots to comment on, made it easier for them to chat lightly instead of talking about the past or the future, and both of them seemed to need it that way. Asher had a good feeling about the new relationship and how it would eventually blossom.

Asher's dad had called the day after he'd come over to report that he'd apologized to Mandy and that they were going to see a couples counselor who specialized in communication. Asher thought that was a good idea even if he couldn't wrap his mind around newlyweds needing that so early in the game. When he'd told Katie about that, she'd said that sometimes people who loved each other just clashed in some areas and needed a little guidance in finding their way together.

Asher wasn't too sure any advice would sink in with his father. His dad meant well, clearly.

And he tried. But the basics of how to coexist with those you loved didn't seem to get inside his head or heart or cells. A couple of days ago, Asher had received a text from his mother while their cruise was docked on their Europe tour, and she'd said that she and her husband weren't speaking at the moment. Asher's heart had sunk. *Here we go again.*

It wasn't until they'd said goodbye that Asher realized the reason his mother had called in the first place was because she needed connection to family, to her son, and she'd reached out. Asher had called her back, asking if she was okay, and she'd said she was sorry to give the impression that the argument was more serious than it was; he'd simply caught her right in the thick of it, and she and David, married seven years, would be just fine. *Our marriage has never been stronger, dopey arguments and all*, his mother had said, and Asher hoped so. But he couldn't be sure of anything when it came to relationships.

And all the conversation did was sour Asher on love and marriage even more than he was already. If his mother's marriage didn't work out, would she actually look for husband number four? Then five?

He shook his head. He and Katie were working out just fine because they'd been sticking to being platonic this past week. They hadn't made any pronouncements, but Katie just seemed to understand that he needed to keep things as they were. Nice and easy. A partnership for their family and for the ranch. No hurt feelings. No expectations.

No sex.

He tried to put his attraction for her out of mind but it was impossible, and even he had to admit that instead of strengthening their partnership, it actually got between them. Instead of sitting next to her on the sofa in their Christmas pj's to watch a movie with a big bowl of popcorn, he'd go check on the goats. Or the twins. Anything to escape how badly he wanted her.

And he'd catch her expression sometimes too. Which made him feel worse. She seemed to realize that he was distancing himself. Because he knew her so well he could see her warring with herself too, telling herself that she needed to give him time and space to work this out with himself.

Which just kept them even farther apart. They didn't talk about these things. They just…understood.

But understanding wasn't giving either of them what they wanted.

Right now, it was just past 1:00 a.m., and Asher heard Declan fussing in the nursery. It was his turn to get up with the goats tomorrow, so Katie would take the middle-of-the-night shift, but he felt unsettled tonight. He needed to see his boys.

Just to sit with that sweet weight in his arms and lean his head back on the rocker.

But when he walked into the nursery, Katie was already there, scooping out Declan from his bassinet. His gaze went to her close-fitting T-shirt and yoga pants, her hair loose past her shoulders. She looked so sexy. He swallowed and froze, wondering how this was going to resolve. Did he say, *The hell with it, let's do this? Let's have a real marriage*, and then end up like his parents, not speaking for days and ending up divorcing?

Or did he control himself for the greater good? A happy future for his family. No problems.

Except he did have a problem.

"I've got this," she said. "Go back to bed. You're getting up super early."

He wanted to say that he was happy right where he was, here with her and the twins. That he was sorry things were so awkward between them. He just wanted to hold her and never let go.

Where they would go from here, how they would get back to what he'd thought they'd have, he had no idea. Everything was different.

But he was the same old Asher. And maybe that was the *real* problem.

Chapter Seventeen

In the morning, Katie had plans to meet Gigi at the gift shop in town to buy presents for her four bridesmaids and maid of honor—Katie herself. Gigi had her eye on seed pearl bracelets and matching drop earrings for all of them and wanted Katie's opinion.

They met at the coffee shop first, and over their cream cheese–slathered bagels and lattes, Katie had filled in her friend on the state of her marriage, which couldn't be more platonic. Her Christmas wish for a real relationship—a romantic, sexual relationship—felt like it was slipping farther and farther out of her hands. Just as she was about to ask Gigi for advice on when and how to talk to Asher about actually taking those baby steps they'd talked about, Gigi's fiancé, Tom, unexpectedly came in, his entire being lighting up at seeing Gigi.

In fact, he stole his fiancée away into the little hallway that led to the restrooms for a kiss that Katie had been able to see. That kiss was so hot it practically curled Katie's toes and she had to look away. She took a long sip of her latte and looked back in time to see Gigi's arms around her fiancé's neck, Tom saying "I love you so much, Cookie Dough," which was one of his pet names for her.

She and Asher didn't have pet names. Unless she counted Freckles back in middle school.

"I want what you have," Katie said when Gigi got back to the table.

"There's one way," Gigi said, then took a bite of her bagel.

Katie had to wait way too long for the answer, which she needed right away.

Finally Gigi swallowed and sipped her drink, then said, "You just have to tell him what you want. And not in the kitchen over coffee or in the barn while sweeping out the straw. I mean in his bedroom. Or yours. Where something can happen."

"But I have told him. And the last time we were together, it backfired on me. He got all turned around at how sex would ruin our relationship."

"From what you've told me, you two have been through a lot, together and separately. With his dad and your mother. With each other. With caring for your children. Life is charging on and he has to know that he can't stay rooted in a past that doesn't make sense for right now."

"*Does* he know that?" Katie asked.

"Of course, he does," Gigi insisted. "He's just trying to pretend it's last year, before the accident, before the ugly words that made you drive off. He wants the relationship you had before you slept together and conceived the twins. Is that possible? Even remotely?"

"No," Katie said. "How could it be?"

"Right. So go tell that stubborn man what you want and need."

Katie finished her coffee. She liked everything Gigi had advised but was it going to change Asher's mind? Probably not.

Defeated before she even tried. She sighed as they got up to leave.

Then again, she thought about what he'd said last week before the dinner with her mother, when she'd been so overwhelmed and had needed to get away—and needed Asher's arms around her. *One step at a time, right? You can't go from nothing to everything just like that. But if you want to have a relationship with your mother, you will. Trust, letting go, a new beginning—all that is going to take time.*

Those words could apply to their relationship too. She'd said as much herself to him about them and their attraction to each other.

She could think and speculate and wonder all she wanted. But Gigi was right—she had to talk to the man. Really talk to him. Let him know what she needed and wanted from their marriage.

A few minutes later they were at the gift shop, and as Gigi bought her bridal party presents, Katie wandered around the store, finding herself in the intimates area in the back. The black satin teddy she'd seen last week, the one with the very revealing, plunging neckline, was calling her name. She'd feel so sexy in that. She could make a move in that. But then what? Asher didn't want her to make a move. Grrr.

"I'd like to buy you that as a wedding gift," said a familiar voice, and Katie whirled around.

Celia Crosby stood there with a playful smile. She pointed at the teddy.

"Oh no, that's okay," Katie said fast, feeling her cheeks burn.

She felt a little closer to Celia since their three get-togethers, especially after the petting zoo with Asher and the twins. The antics of the animals, particularly the babies, gave them a lot to laugh about, and Katie had had to admit afterward to Asher that her mother truly seemed a changed woman and that she was enchanted with the twins. But still, they were just getting to know each other.

"Doing some Christmas shopping?" Katie asked to change the subject.

Celia nodded. "I'm on my fifteen-minute break from the bakery so I'm just looking around, really. I'm lucky I ran into you. Will you let me buy that nightgown for you as a wedding gift? I'd really love to."

"There's really no point because Asher and I are platonic," Katie blurted out, then froze. Why had she said that? The only person she'd told about her and Asher was Gigi, who she trusted with her life. She didn't trust her mother, not yet. So why had she shared something so personal? Something that had her tied up in knots too?

"Platonic?" Celia repeated. "But you're married." Her gaze went to the silver band on Katie's finger, right below the engagement ring.

Katie bit her lip and explained about his grandmother's will and the ranch. Then the night with Asher that led to him ending their first engagement a year ago. Her driving away. The accident. Coming home. The new proposal. And the platonic marriage. With a few detours to amazing sex that had Asher tied in knots. She added what

Gigi advised. Which was what had brought her over here to the lingerie section, unsure what to do.

"Oh, Katie, I had no idea," Celia said. "The love between you and Asher is palpable. I mean, you can actually see it and feel it in the air. That wonderful day at the petting zoo—the way he looked at you."

"We've always loved each other, though—like best friends for decades. That's nothing new."

"Sounds like he's been trying hard not to acknowledge that your love for each other has grown leaps and bounds," Celia said. "But Gigi's right—he can't."

"He has been, though."

"Maybe you've been letting him?" Celia said. "Giving him *too* much space? I say stop doing that. Put on the good pressure. In that teddy," she added, nodding her chin at it.

Katie couldn't help the smile. "You really think so?"

"I really do. He's stuck right now, Katie. And you can get him unstuck. No one knows better than I do at how stuck people can get in old ways of looking at things. Fear of the future and all that." Gigi glanced at her watch. "Oh gosh, my break is over in four minutes. I'd better get back. You can do anything you set your mind to, Katie. I believe that more than anything."

Katie felt that right in her heart. "Thanks, Mom," she said and then gasped. That was the first time she'd called her mother *Mom* in decades.

Celia's eyes got misty. She reached over and hugged Katie and Katie hugged her back.

Katie watched her leave, not even realizing Gigi had walked over.

"Did I hear you just call your mother *Mom*?" Gigi asked.

"I did. I actually really did."

"If you could get *there*, Katie Crosby Dawson, then Asher could get *here*," she said, grabbing the sexy negligee from the hanger and marching it up to the counter.

When the salesclerk informed her that the woman who'd just left had paid for it already Katie gasped for the second time that morning.

New beginnings, she thought. For me and my mother. For me and Asher.

"Go get your man," Gigi said. "Tonight's the night. Or afternoon." She wiggled her eyebrows.

Maybe it *was*.

On her way back to the ranch, the black negligee in its box on the passenger seat making her both nervous and excited, Katie stopped at the mailbox on the main road. There was the usual junk mail, a couple of bills, a little package from Mandy's spa and a very official-looking envelope from the State of Wyoming. *Ooh*, Katie thought, *it must be our marriage certificate.*

Between that and the sexy nightie, Asher would certainly see that it was time to make their marriage officially official. A real marriage. With all the emotional ups and downs. With great sex and even nights on the couch, if an argument or two led to that, knowing they could trust each other to argue or not see eye to eye on everything and that they would work through it because they loved each other and wanted to be together.

She turned down the drive to the ranch, butterflies letting loose inside her stomach as the barn and then the ranch house came into view. The goats were in the pasture, Eloisa and Mimi on logs. Katie smiled at them, grabbed her package and the mail and hurried in the house.

"How was shopping?" Asher asked as he came down the stairs. "I just put the twins down for their nap."

"I'll go up in a minute and say a silent hi," she said with a smile. "Shopping was great. Gigi bought her bridal party gifts and even I got a little something." She held up the bag with a mischievous smile.

She made a decision that while the twins had their hour-and-a-half nap, she'd make good use of the time. She smiled again—feeling it in her toes and her belly button. A delicious set of goose bumps ran up her spine.

"And look at this," she said, tossing the mail and package on the coffee table. "Very official letter from the State of Wyoming. I'll bet it's our marriage certificate." She ripped open the envelope and pulled out a letter on state stationery.

"Huh," she said. "It's not our marriage certificate."

"What is it?" he asked, stepping alongside her to read it with her.

As Katie read, her stomach flip-flopped. *"What?"*

She read aloud, "'Unfortunately, as the marriage license was not signed by two witnesses in addition to the officiant, the marriage is not legal in the state of Wyoming...'"

"In addition to the officiant?" Asher repeated.

"Oh heck," Katie said. "Mandy must have thought that the two witnesses included her as officiant."

"We're not married?" Asher asked, staring at her.

We're not married, she thought, tears stinging the backs of her eyes.

She shook her head and dropped the letter on the coffee table, sinking down onto the sofa. "I can't believe this. If only the twins could have signed their names," she added on a half smile that turned right into a frown.

"Me either," he said. "But it's okay. We've got over a week till Christmas. We'll just get married again," he said with something of a smile. "Mandy and John will have something to laugh about—or cry about—for the rest of their lives, how we had to have *two* weddings because of them. And we can have a bigger ceremony this time. Invite family and friends. Mandy can officiate again. There'll be lots of people to ask to join my dad in signing as a witness. Your mom, maybe."

It was a nice thought. Very nice. And a few days ago, Katie would have jumped at the chance to have a wedding with friends and family—and yes, her mother.

But it was one thing to legally wed in order to have a platonic marriage—with his dad and Mandy and the twins as their sole guests. It was another to do it in front of everyone they cared about, everyone who cared about them.

It was another to do so knowing what she did now. That she couldn't go on like this.

"I'll be right back," she said.

"Going to see the twins?" he asked, looking at her with concern. "You okay, Katie?"

"I do need to go see the twins," she said. "And then there's something I need to do. It'll just take me five minutes."

"Okay. Then we'll figure this out. No worries, okay?" He reached for her hand and gave it a squeeze.

Ha, she thought as she headed up the stairs with her bag containing the nightie. No worries.

In her bedroom, Katie slid off her jeans and sweater. Then her bra and underwear. She took the negligee out of the box, snipped off the tags and then moved over to the corner to the full-length standing mirror. She slipped the teddy over her head and let it fall, loving the silky material and how it felt against her bare skin. She looked at her reflection, happy with how it skimmed her body. The low-cut neckline would certainly capture Asher's attention—even at just after twelve thirty in the afternoon. And the teddy was short enough to be risqué without showing a thing. Except a lot of leg.

She smiled and twirled around. She knew she didn't need a sexy outfit to do her work for her here. Either Asher would be on board with moving into their future or he wouldn't, and looking sexy, especially in the middle of the day, wasn't going to matter. But Katie, coming downstairs in this negligee, said loud and clear that she wanted a romantic relationship. And that moving forward—getting married again—meant being as real as the new marriage certificate would be.

Here goes everything, she thought.

Katie had wished and prayed for a lot over

the course of her life, since young childhood, but she'd never wanted anything more than she wanted *this*. A real relationship with the man she loved, the father of her children.

A real marriage.

She left the room, stopping in the hallway to give her hair a shake upside down and flip it back over like she was in a music video. She headed downstairs, and halfway there she could see Asher in the living room, going through the mail.

"I'm back," she called, hoping she was smiling and not showing how nervous she felt.

He turned and stared at her, and she saw his Adam's apple move. Which meant he was affected by what he saw. "That is very sexy," he said, his gaze traveling—just as she wanted. He lingered on the plunging neckline, then down to how the silky satin skimmed her hips, then to the swishy hemline high up on her thighs. He swallowed again, his eyes moving up to hers. "Wow," he whispered. "Wow."

"That's what I was hoping you'd say," she whispered back.

She walked up to him and took both of his hands, her eyes on his. "I'm just going to come right out and say this. I love you. I've loved you forever, yes. But I love you in every way. I love you the way you're supposed to love the person you marry. I want us to move forward with a real relationship, a real marriage. I want to share a bedroom. I want us to share in the ups and downs of life, the beautiful and scary road of parenthood, the bumps of a couple who loves hard. I want it all, Asher."

He put a finger under her chin but then took a step back. "I—" he began, but then stopped. He was looking into her eyes but she had the feeling it was to keep them off her body in the teddy. "Katie—" He stopped as if searching for what he wanted to say. He turned away for a moment, then back to her. "There's a week left for us to marry to keep the ranch. Why don't we just redo the ceremony and then sit with this and..." But he trailed off because there was no *and*. There was nothing really to say.

Her heart plummeted to her stomach. To her toes. To the floor. "Do you love me, Asher?"

"You know I do, Katie. Which is why I think we need to move a lot slower. Not jump into a real marriage when we've been friends our whole lives."

"For how long?" she asked, feeling herself getting choked up. "A couple of months? A couple of years? Or do we just stay married for the year and then go our separate ways while co-parenting the twins?"

"No, I—I don't know. I just know this is too

fast. We'll end up like my parents. Neither of their marriages is working out. Number three for my mom, number four for my dad. Let's just wait until we're solid, Katie."

She felt her eyes widen. "Solid? You can't get more solid than we are. Are you really going to let fear of breaking up keep us apart? From really loving each other? Asher."

"We..." He turned away, staring at the Christmas tree, then looking out the sliding glass doors. "We have an arrangement. For the sake of our children. For their ranch. Getting married was always about that. Not about *us*."

"I need *us* to enter the equation. I need our marriage to be about us too."

"It was never about us," he pointed out, and the tears stung again. She blinked them back hard.

"So this is what you want to teach the twins? To avoid risk for fear of failure? Unlikely failure, given what we mean to each other and for how long."

"That's not fair, Katie."

"Our friendship has progressed, whether you can handle it or not," she said. "It's not the same. *We're* not the same."

"We are, though. At heart, we're Katie and Asher, best friends as we've always been. And we can't jeopardize that. For the twins. Because when we end up arguing and slamming doors and sleeping on the couch and then taking off and then divorcing, it's Declan and Dylan who will hurt the worst."

"So I guess we won't be teaching them how to ride a two-wheeler when they're six years old in case they fall off and get seriously injured. That's how you want us to live our lives?"

"We're talking about us. You and me. I think we should be friends as we always have been. As we agreed to be when you came back."

"Well, I can't continue like this, Ash. I can't. I've tried. I need more from you. And not just for me. For you and for the twins."

He looked so pained that she stopped talking and dropped down on the love seat.

"I will marry you all over again for the ranch and so the twins can have their family legacy," she said. "But our relationship, our friendship won't be the same. It can't be because it isn't. We'll live separate lives till the year is up and then we'll go our separate ways, co-parenting by always putting the boys first."

"Katie—"

She stood up, blinking back tears, and then ran upstairs into her room and shut the door. She took off the teddy and put it back in the box and slid it under her bed, then put on a long-sleeved

T-shirt and yoga pants and collapsed on her bed. She stared up at the ceiling, then wrapped her arms around herself, getting no comfort at all.

Chapter Eighteen

They tiptoed around each other for the rest of the day—and night. Asher felt like hell. His head was pounding and pain reliever barely helped it. His chest felt like someone had kicked him hard, many times. And his stomach was full of sludge and churning. If he didn't know what heartache felt like from losing Katie last year, he would have thought he had the flu.

After their conversation in the living room, he'd gone up to his bedroom and alternated between pacing and staring out the window. Every time he heard Katie's door open, he jumped, but then he'd hear another door open and close and he would realize she'd gone into the nursery and certainly didn't want him in there with her.

After an hour of that, he'd spent a long time in the barn, taking care of the goats, getting them inside and fed. When he came back in, Katie had been by the front door with the twins in their stroller, and a terrible fear had gripped him. Turned out she was just going to Gigi's for dinner and he shouldn't wait up.

After that, the house was so quiet he couldn't stand it. He'd put on Christmas music, but it didn't suit his mood. He ate a bowl of sugary cereal standing up at the counter and then scrubbed the sink and thought about tackling the refrigerator but even he had a limit. She wasn't back by ten and he texted her to make sure she was okay.

I'll be home in a half hour, she texted back. The twins have long been asleep. We'll talk in the morning about how to proceed.

The thing was, he knew he was blowing something big, that this was his fault, even though he tried to home in on their initial agreement of being platonic. They *had* moved on, their friendship *wasn't* the same. He knew that. He just didn't like it, wasn't comfortable with it.

He was in his bedroom when he heard her car pull in. He went out to help her bring the twins in, but they didn't speak other than polite chitchat about her time with Gigi and if the twins needed to be changed. Then there were polite smiles and after telling him she'd take night wakings, she didn't say another word. Once they had the boys in their bassinets, she'd left and gone into her room, the door closing behind her.

He'd spent a terrible night tossing and turning. When Asher woke up in the morning—after his worst night's sleep since Katie had come back— he could hear sounds from downstairs. He went to the door and opened it. Katie was talking to the twins, telling them about how in a few months, they'd get to try scrambled eggs and all sorts of delicious breakfasts. Her voice sounded like forced cheerfulness.

This wasn't how it was supposed to be. Exactly the opposite.

He took a quick shower and got dressed in a Henley and jeans and then headed downstairs, desperate to see her face, needing to see his sons.

"Morning," she said when he appeared in the kitchen doorway. "I'll pour you a mug of coffee. I just brewed a fresh pot."

"Thanks," he said, and she barely looked at him when she handed it to him.

The twins were in their high chairs, Declan playing with a rattle in the shape of a candy corn and Dylan pressing on a foam block.

"So," she said, sitting down at the table with her own coffee. "I figure we should make a plan for the redo of the ceremony. We could either go back to the spa or have your dad and Mandy come here, and I can ask Gigi to be our second witness."

"Whichever you think," he said.

"Let's just do it here. In the living room. Make it quick. Just to be safe and ensure the certificate is mailed well before the deadline of Christmas Day, I'm thinking we should do it tonight so that we just get it over with, not have it hanging over our heads. I remember Mandy mentioning that Mondays were always slow days at the spa. They could drive up after five, we'll do the ceremony and they can head home within an hour. Gigi gets off work at five, so that'll work for her."

Asher could see she was on the verge of tears. "I'll call my dad and let him know what happened with the witnesses thing and see if they can come tonight. I'm sure that'll be fine."

Nothing was fine, though.

He went into the living room and called his father, who answered right away. Asher explained about the missing witness signature and how they needed to redo the ceremony. His dad called that out to Mandy, practically blowing out Asher's eardrum, and then Mandy got on the phone, full of apologies, and how could she have missed that, and of course they'd drive down tonight to have the new ceremony.

"Bring a healing crystal," he heard himself saying before he could catch himself. "Something to turn back time, if that's a thing."

Mandy was quiet for a moment. "I've got just the one," she said.

But Asher knew only a certain superhero could turn back time. And anyway, he knew there was no going back.

In the kitchen, he told Katie they were set for six o'clock and she texted Gigi, who texted back that she'd be there with her permanent marker to sign the certificate.

"I guess I can wear this," she said, looking down at her pink T-shirt and yoga pants.

"What really matters is the marriage, so sure," he said. "I could wear this," he added, waving a hand down himself.

She twisted her lips. "I guess we should try to act like there's nothing wrong, though. So we should probably wear what we wore the first time around."

He nodded. "Agreed. It's a lot to heap on them."

And so at five that night, Asher was up in his room putting on his suit and shiny black shoes, staring at himself in the mirror and wondering what the hell he was going to do to fix this.

Mandy and John arrived early at five thirty, Mandy in a fancy tweed suit and heels and John

268 SANTA'S TWIN SURPRISE

in a navy suit. A cry came from upstairs almost immediately so Asher and his dad headed upstairs to see to the twins, Mandy tossing John a burp cloth to protect his suit.

Mandy apologized again for missing such a basic requirement and not realizing the officiant couldn't count herself among the two witnesses, and Katie assured her it was fine, that the fact that they weren't actually married and had to redo the wedding had finally made them both realize a few things.

"Like that I need more than this," Katie said, bursting into tears and covering her face with her hands.

"Oh hey, it's gonna be okay," Mandy said, pulling Katie into her arms for a hug. "I guess Asher wasn't kidding when he asked me to bring a healing crystal that could turn back time. How far back do we need to go? Did you guys have an argument this afternoon?"

Katie swiped under her eyes. "Teenage years. Maybe early twenties."

Mandy looked confused.

Katie took her arm and led the way upstairs, hurrying into her bedroom so if Asher and his father came out, they wouldn't see her tear-streaked face. She closed the door and then dropped down on her bed, Mandy sitting on the edge. "When we met two Novembers ago, you know that Asher and I were just friends. Best friends. That's all we've ever been. But I've been in love with him for as long as I can remember." She explained about the terms of his grandmother's will, then everything that had happened since. "And when I told him yesterday that I can't go on like this, we found ourselves at a stalemate."

Mandy opened her purse and withdrew an intensely green crystal. "Here. Put this in your palm and hold on to it for thirty seconds. It's malachite. The stone of transformation. It's to bring your heart into focus. Your father is giving one to Asher right about now."

Katie sighed, holding the crystal tight. "I'm not sure anything will work on him."

"So you told him what you wanted and he's still stuck ten years in the past?" Mandy asked.

Katie nodded. "I love him so much that I want to give him what he wants—a platonic marriage. But I can't. I honestly don't know how he can stand it."

"It's just fear, Katie. His father is in the same rickety boat but it's also sprung a leak. The Dawson men are going to have to figure out that they'll need to let go to get what they really want. *Us.*"

"But will they?" Katie asked.

"You hold on to that crystal, dear," Mandy said with a comforting and assured nod.

Katie wasn't sure how it would help, but she'd try anything at this point.

* * *

"Now, Asher, I'm gonna be honest," his father said as he tilted his head left, then right, looking Asher over from where he was leaning against the wall by the window. "You look like hell. Hardly like a man who's about to get married. Again."

Asher sank down on his bed, probably wrinkling his suit pants. "Now it's *my* relationship that's in trouble. Big trouble."

"What? You and Katie? You two are made for each other. Peanut butter and jelly. Cookies and milk. Steak and roasted potatoes. Coffee and a lot of sugar."

"I haven't exactly been honest about us," Asher said, leaning his head back. "You ready?"

"Lay it on me," John said, grabbing the desk chair and bringing it over to face the bed.

Asher told him everything. From Gram dying to the will to the terrible argument he and Katie had had before her "death" to the four of them living like a family to this afternoon's conversation. "I screwed up bad but I don't know how to get past my own self. What the hell am I doing? I think that, and I leap up to go save the best thing that's ever happened to me, but then it's like my legs turn to lead and I can't breathe. Marriage doesn't work out. You know that better than anyone. No offense."

"Sure they do, Asher," his dad said. "Yes, I had

three previous misses and I haven't been doing as well as I should on this fourth one. But Mandy is the world to me and I'm not letting her get away. I don't know how to change, but I will to keep her."

Huh. His father had never really said anything like that before. He'd said he'd work on himself and try, but admitting he didn't know how and still would make it happen—that was new.

"The problem here is that you don't *want* to change, Asher. You want to stay in the rosy past that doesn't exist anymore. Thing is, there's no Declan and Dylan in that rosy past. They're here *now*. The here and now. Just like Katie is. She's right about the two of you not being the same people, the same friends. You're not. Think about all you've been through, all you've weathered. That's who you are. A couple who's been through it all, has these two beautiful babies and can get through anything. Even your stubborn, guarded head and heart."

"But what do I do about it?" Asher asked. "How do I get past it?"

"You just have to. Just like you told me *I* had to." He looked out the window for a moment, then back at Asher. "I've been afraid of losing everything my entire life. It's why I push everything away. Starting with the goats when I was a kid. With this ranch. With my relationships. With you.

It's why I never got another damned dog after I lost the one I loved so much as a kid. *Fear.*"

"Did you like the ranch at one point?" he asked his dad.

"Yeah. When I was very young. Before my parents let me bring in the dog, I used to talk to the goats. Tell them everything. But when I lost that dog, my best friend, something changed in me. Hard. It had control of me and I thought it was a good trait so I let it lead me. All it did was make me miserable. I wouldn't get close to anyone. Not even when I was married. Of course those relationships didn't work out. I didn't want them to. I didn't realize that then."

Asher stared at his father, realizing how much everything he was saying made sense.

"But Mandy's wise and has a way of reading me," John continued. "And there's just something so special about her, Ash. You know that movie with Jack Nicholson who's a total malcontent and that nice blonde waitress who demands a compliment from him, and he says she makes him want to be a better man? That's how Mandy makes me feel. I know I've got some stuff to work on and I'm in my late fifties. But I have to change. I have to be a better man. And for Mandy, I'm going to."

"I bet you will, Dad. I really believe that." And he did.

"Oh, I was supposed to give you this." He

reached into his pocket and pulled out a small green stone. "It's supposed to transform you."

Asher smiled. "I definitely need that." He held the stone tight, then took a deep breath. "Katie's the best thing that ever happened to me. And all I've done since she came back to me is push her away. Am I nuts?"

"Nah. Just scared of losing her. I get it. I'm not losing Mandy because of me, Asher. That would be the dumbest thing in the world."

Asher laughed. "Yeah, it would." He gave the green stone another squeeze. He could hear the doorbell ring and glanced at his phone on the bedside table. "That must be Gigi, our other witness. Katie's friend."

"Well, why don't Mandy and I go let her in while you go talk to your wife slash bride-to-be. We'll get the boys ready for the ceremony in their tuxedo pj's."

Asher stood up and before his dad turned to head out, Asher called him back. "Thanks," he said, pulling him into a bear hug. "I love you, Dad."

His father's eyes got teary. "I love you too. I don't think we've said that to each other in decades."

"Well, we're both changing men now."

"Got that right." With that, his father left the room. He heard him dash downstairs and the sound of Gigi's voice, then footsteps on the stairs. Then he heard his dad, Mandy and Gigi chatting about the twins and the nursery door opening.

He headed down the hall and knocked on Katie's door.

"Come on in, Gigi," she called.

He opened the door. Katie was in her beautiful wedding dress and heels. "It's actually me."

"Oh," she said, sitting back down on her bed.

She had something in her hand. He hoped like hell it wasn't her engagement ring that she was planning on flinging at him. He peered into the side of her fist and saw something glowing green.

"I've got one too," he said, opening his hand. "It's working."

"Is it?" she said, putting hers down on the bedside table.

"Everything you said is right, Katie. I'm afraid of losing you and I can't be anymore. There is no before anymore. There's just now. And the future. Do you know that my dad said something that turned my head around?"

"What was it?" she asked, and he could see the wary hope on her beautiful face.

"He said I couldn't go back to the Katie and Asher of before and that I wouldn't want to because there would be no Declan and Dylan. Do you know that I never thought of that?"

"Huh. I'm not sure I thought of it that way either."

"I am scared of losing you, Katie. But yes, I
love you more than anything. And I want you
more than anything. Fighting against how much
I want you has been a nightmare."

She laughed. "For me too."

"Will you marry me again, Katie Crosby Dawson? In every sense of the word?"

She flung herself at him and he wrapped his
arms around her. "I absolutely will."

"Let's go get married—for real this time."

Epilogue

A week and a half later, Katie and Asher threw a big wedding reception/Christmas party in the ballroom at the lodge of the Dawson Family Guest Ranch. The place was decked out for the holiday, lights twinkling everywhere, an enormous tree by the huge arched windows. All the Dawson cousins were there, including cousins Asher rarely saw—Colt Dawson, his wife, Allie, and their baby son, Ryder. They lived on an alpaca farm a few hours away, and Katie's eyes had lit up at the invitation to visit. And then there was Gavin Dawson and his wife, Lily, and their baby, Micah, who owned the huge Wild Canyon Ranch about fifteen minutes away. Katie had made plans to have them over to dinner, thrilled that their family got bigger and bigger.

Two Dawsons who weren't here? Mandy and John. Asher was happy to know that they were actually back in Las Vegas, renewing their vows at the same Elvis Presley chapel by the same impersonator and taking a mini honeymoon.

There was a theme for this daytime party—goofiest Christmas sweater—so everyone had tried to outdo one another. Asher wore the one Katie had bought him as a wedding present, "North Pole Daddy" across the front with the earnest Santa and cartoon reindeer and elves around the neckline and hem. Katie, holding Dylan, was chatting with her mom, who held Declan, both in matching bright sweaters with candy canes all over them. Goofy, but certainly not going to win their annual contest. Asher had that in the bag, and it had been Katie who'd won it for him.

Katie had spent a lot of time with her mom these past days, and Celia had looked very happy to be invited over for Christmas Eve dinner tomorrow night and to spend Christmas Day with them. Katie had mentioned that her mom had been chatting a lot today with Chief Harringer, who'd been widowed for years. They'd been seen dancing together twice, and Katie said maybe they'd *both* be joining them for Christmas this year.

"Great party," his cousin Ford said, coming to stand on one side of him while his cousin Rex stood on the other.

"I've had way too much eggnog," Rex said, patting his stomach over his Christmas sweater, which featured the Grinch, red hearts shooting out of his chest getting bigger and bigger as he held his little dog wearing tiny antlers instead of the huge ones.

"Oh, the Grinch's dog just reminded me," Asher said. "Want to see the newest member of the Crosby-Dawson household?" He held up his phone, a photo of their new Australian shepherd mix, Noelle, wearing her red-and-green collar. The adorable brown-and-white dog, a stray the animal shelter had found in Brewster, had joined their family just days ago. Noelle always looked like she was smiling, and Asher and Katie were having fun spoiling her rotten.

"Merry Christmas, Asher," Ford said with a smile at the photo and then at Asher. "I don't think I've ever meant that more."

His cousins gave him a clap on the back and were pulled away by colleagues to the dancing area, which was packed with little kids shaking their hips to "Frosty the Snowman."

Katie danced her way over to Asher with each baby on a hip. Asher took Declan, snuggling the boy close.

"My every Christmas wish has come true," Katie said, reaching up to kiss Asher on the lips. She touched the locket he'd given her, which held a tiny photo of the twins. She and Asher were now sharing a bedroom, truly sharing a life.

"Mine too," he said. "Ones I didn't even know I had." *That* was the truth.

And then the song "Merry Christmas Baby" came on, and they headed to the dance floor with their twins, Asher's own heart ten times bigger.

* * * * *